Will Somebody *Please* Marry My Sister?

Other Apple Paperbacks
by Eth Clifford

Help! I'm a Prisoner in the Library

I Hate Your Guts, Ben Brooster

Just Tell Me When We're Dead!

Leah's Song
(original title: *The Man Who Sang in the Dark*)

Scared Silly

The Summer of the Dancing Horse

Will Somebody *Please* Marry My Sister?

ETH CLIFFORD

Interior illustrations
by Ellen Eagle

AN
APPLE
PAPERBACK

SCHOLASTIC INC.
New York Toronto London Auckland Sydney

In memory of Rita Stark,
whose warmth and wit
and caring friendship
will never be forgotten

ISBN 0-590-46624-0

 Published by Scholastic Inc., 730 Broadway, New York, NY 10003, by arrangement with Houghton Mifflin Company.

12 11 10 9 8 7 6 5 4 3 2 1 3 4 5 6 7 8/9

Printed in the U.S.A. 28

First Scholastic printing, December 1993

Contents

1

Who Makes the Rules?

"Rules! Rules! Rules! Who made up this rule anyway?" Abel Stoner exploded. He ran his hand through his mop of gold-red hair as if he intended to yank it all out in frustration. His eyes blazed in anger.

"So ask me another one," Grandma Birdie replied tranquilly. "How should I know? All I can tell you is that it was always a rule, as far back as I can remember. A younger sister cannot get married before the older sister, no matter what."

Grandma Birdie, who wasn't birdlike at all, took a hearty sip from her second cup of coffee. At seven o'clock in the morning, she claimed, she needed lots of coffee to wake up properly. She was a short woman, with gray hair caught up in a knot at the top of her head. Her eyes twinkled in good humor as she regarded her grandson.

"Who believes in old-fashioned rules anymore?" Abel insisted. "Grandma, this is 1925. And you're living in Brooklyn, New York, in the United States of America. We don't have rules in America."

Grandma Birdie slapped a slab of fresh whipped butter against a seeded roll.

"Is that a fact?" she asked, after her second bite of roll. "You think, because you're twelve years old and going to seventh grade, that you know everything? Well, Mr. Know-It-All, let's talk about baseball."

Abel was surprised. Baseball? He loved the game, could rattle off the batting average of every major player, and played baseball out on the street every chance he got. But what did his grandmother know about the game? She knew more than he realized, as he discovered when she said, "Tell me something. Suppose a batter decides he doesn't feel like using a bat to hit the ball. Suppose he decides to use a rolling pin instead?"

She grinned at his expression.

"A *rolling pin*?" He couldn't believe he'd heard that.

Grandma Birdie raced on, like an express train passing a local station.

"Suppose a batter doesn't want to bother with first base? Suppose he just goes to second base? Maybe he — "

Abel interrupted swiftly. "That's just plain ridiculous. You *have* to go to first base . . ."

"Why?" she asked with an innocent look. "Who says so?"

"It's the rule! That's why."

"Aha! You see, Abel? It's the rule. There are rules for everything. Case closed."

"Are you two at it again?" a voice inquired.

Abel didn't have to turn his head to know that his eighteen-year-old sister, Annie, had entered the room. Like Grandma Birdie, she was short. Her boyfriend, Bruce Jonas, called her petite. He also said Annie was pleasingly plump.

With her large dark brown eyes and her shiny dark hair, and her usually jolly nature, she could pass for pretty. Abel was willing to admit that much. Poor Bruce. Abel shook his head. If Bruce could only see Annie first thing in the morning. If he only knew how Annie monopolized the one bathroom in this two-bedroom apartment.

Right now, however, what was important to Abel was having Annie on his side.

"Why don't you ask Annie how she feels about that dumb older-sister rule?" he asked.

Got you there, Abel decided, grinning. When Abel smiled, the mass of freckles on his face seemed to flow right across his nose. His eyes crinkled until they almost disappeared.

Grandma Birdie refused to ask. She knew what An-

nie would say. Instead she watched with dismay as Annie ignored the rolls and reached for her second large piece of Danish pastry.

"Seven o'clock in the morning you're eating *cake*?" she cried, as if this wasn't a familiar morning ritual.

"Oh no," Abel agreed in mock horror. "Cake? Of course not! There's a rule, right, Grandma?"

"What's the matter with you?" Annie wondered.

Grandma Birdie began to push away from the table. "We were talking about rules, as usual. Abel still doesn't believe in them."

"I think a rule that says a younger sister can't get married until her older sister does first is dumb. That's all. *D-u-m-b,* stupid." Abel leaned back in his chair and glared at his grandmother.

Annie did a little glaring of her own.

"For once in his life, Grandma, Abel is right. Suppose Ruthie never gets married."

"I don't ever want you to say that again. Your sister is not going to be an old maid, understand?"

"She's twenty-six," Annie reminded her grandmother. "Twenty — six!" she repeated, drawing out the words for extra emphasis.

"So? Her life isn't exactly over yet. Trust me."

Grandma Birdie walked to the front door, yanked it open, turned to warn, "The store opens at seven-thirty. *Sharp*," then slammed the door shut behind her. She always became furious when she was reminded that her oldest granddaughter had reached the age of twenty-six with no prospect of a bridegroom.

Abel knew, however, that his grandmother's thoughts would switch from Ruth the moment she stepped into the store downstairs. She opened it eagerly in the morning, and closed it reluctantly in the evening.

It had begun as two small separate stores. On one side, Grandpa Stoner had run a coffee shop. Large burlap sacks were open at the top to display many kinds of coffee beans. There were no signs, but Grandpa Stoner knew them all. Supremo from Colombia, American from Brazil, Blue Mountain from Jamaica, and Arabica from Ethiopia.

Grandpa Stoner had a huge map of the world on one wall and would point out the countries from which the coffee beans came, whether his customers wanted to know or not. Behind a long counter were assorted sizes of brown bags, a huge coffee grinder, and a small cash register.

Next door was a pastry shop. Here Grandma Birdie shone. Everything was baked either by Grandma Birdie or her baker-helper, Himmel. He was a small, irritable man who baked through the night so there could be fresh rolls and breads and pastries when the store opened early in the morning. No one, not even

Grandma Birdie, knew whether Himmel had a first name. No one knew whether he had a family.

Himmel slept on a cot in a storeroom a little larger than a closet. When he took a break from his labors, he boiled coffee in a chipped enamel pot, ate his own fresh rolls, sat at a tiny table, and read his newspaper.

Everything he read made him angry.

"Blockhead. Liar," he shouted at the editorials.

He shook the paper with fury when he took exception to a news report. "Garbage," he yelled. "For this they pay you good money?"

Himmel, in fact, had a wonderful time hating the whole world, except Grandma Birdie. They got along splendidly. She ignored his complaints; he admired her brilliance in creating new and delicious recipes.

"A genius," he told her often. "You're a just plain genius."

Between them, they produced the finest, most luscious specialties in all of Brooklyn.

After Grandpa Stoner died, Grandma Birdie had the wall removed between the two stores and continued Grandpa Stoner's great tradition of freshly ground coffee.

Abel and Annie loved their grandmother, but right now, staring at the door she had slammed, they were angry. How could she go on ignoring how they felt because of her fixed notion about the older-sister rule?

"Grandma and her rules," Abel muttered. "It will take dynamite to get her to change her mind. She's got to be the most stubborn person in the whole world."

Annie set her lips in a grim line. "I can be stubborn, too, Abel. Bruce and I want to get married. We're not going to wait forever for Miss High-and-Mighty Ruthie to change her mind."

Abel looked at his sister hopefully. "Do you have an idea?"

She shook her head. "Not yet, but maybe I'll think of something. Maybe you'll think of something."

Abel stared into space, lost in thought. Finally he said, "Things would have been so different if Mom and Pop hadn't died."

A car crash had taken the lives of his parents and grandfather. How could people be alive one minute and gone forever the next?

"I bet Mom and Pop wouldn't have had dumb rules. I bet they would have made sure I had my own room."

Annie sighed. "What's the use of wondering what they would have done?"

"It isn't fair, that's all. It just isn't fair."

Annie took her brother's hand and squeezed it gently. Then she reminded him, "But think how lucky we were in another way, Abel. What would we have done without Grandma?"

She had taken the children — Ruth, age 16, Annie,

8, and Abel, 2, to live with her. Space was limited in her small two-bedroom apartment, so Annie shared Grandma Birdie's room, Abel slept on the couch in the living room, and Ruth had the second bedroom.

Ruth, Grandma explained, was in high school. She needed space to study and do homework and special projects. That seemed fair to Annie, who was in third grade, and very impressed with her almost grown-up sister.

"Some day Ruth will be a schoolteacher, or a nurse," Grandma Birdie said. "Our Ruth is a very ambitious girl."

Ruth, however, had a different goal in mind.

"I'm going to be a doctor," she told them. "Wait and see."

"Ruthie, sweetheart." Grandma Birdie was appalled. "You don't understand. Girls don't *become* doctors. They *marry* doctors." She shook her head. "Do you know any women doctors? Of course not," she answered her own question. "Besides, even if there were, who would go to a woman doctor?"

Ruth tossed back her red-brown hair, which she wore short, with bangs across her forehead. She fixed her grandmother with a determined look and said, "I've made up my mind."

She never changed it. And now she was Ruth Belle Stoner, M.D.

It was unheard of, of course, for an unmarried woman, even a doctor, to live alone, so Ruth continued to occupy her room at home. She rented two small offices over the corner drugstore. Each time she entered the door that led upstairs, Ruth would stop to polish the brass sign that read "Ruth Belle Stoner, M.D.," so that it gleamed and beckoned to prospective patients.

And that was the way it was, and would be, Abel thought morosely. Ruth was still in firm possession of her room. She didn't want to marry, and she seemed content with things just the way they'd always been.

Annie and Bruce were so very much in love, but the rules said they couldn't marry until Ruth did.

And what about Abel? How long would he go on sleeping on the couch? When would he have a space he could call his own?

How he envied Bruce, whose father and mother owned the butcher shop two doors down the street. They lived in the same kind of two-bedroom apartment, but Bruce had his own room. His parents didn't mind the tennis racket hanging on the wall, or the ice skates dangling from a nail, or the catcher's mitt on top of the clothes he never seemed to hang away in his closet, or even the bicycle pushed into a corner.

"When I get my own room, it will be exactly like

this," Abel said, each time he visited. "Well, not exactly, maybe. What I really want is this."

He ran his hand lovingly over the amateur radio equipment on a shelf that served Bruce as a desk.

"I know, Abel. You want to be a ham, too. Just like me."

Abel glanced up at the cards spread out on the wall, sent by hams from around the world. He longed for a display like that.

"Some day, Abel. Wait and see. At least we've got you started on the Morse code. Have you been practicing?"

Had Abel been practicing? Dots and dashes constantly flashed through his mind as he repeated the alphabet to himself. *A* was *dit dah*. *Dit* for a dot, *dah* for a dash. SOS, the call for help, was three dots, three dashes, and three dots.

Yes, in his room, he'd have his amateur radio equipment, his own call letters (Bruce's were W2CDV), cards from other hams, and a huge map of the world he'd mark with crayons to show where all his cards came from, just for him in his little corner of Brooklyn, New York, the United States of America.

"CQ, CQ," he could imagine himself tapping out. CQ meant "anyone who hears me, please answer."

And hams would respond. And they would drop in to visit, just as they did with Bruce. They'd look up, see Abel's aerial on the roof, and ring his doorbell.

"Just passing by," they would say, and then they'd talk, share information, and welcome him as one of a special group of people, the way they did now with Bruce.

If he had his own room. No. Not if. When!

Oh, to get Ruth to marry somebody — anybody. Then Annie would be happy, and he'd have a private space of his own. *A private space of his own.* The six most beautiful words in the English language.

"Listen, Annie," Abel said, as his sister was about to go downstairs to the coffee shop. "I'm going to find a husband for Ruthie. Just you wait and see."

Annie paused, her hand on the doorknob, to give her brother a long, skeptical look.

"Wonderful, Abel. You do that. Find her a husband. Then tell me how you plan to get Ruthie to marry him."

As she began to run down the steps, Abel yelled after her, "I can be just as stubborn as anybody else around here. Ruthie is going to get married, whether she wants to or not."

2

A Tremendous Idea

During the summer months, Abel had a number of jobs. Mornings, he worked at Mr. Pincher's grocery store in the middle of the block. Afternoons, he ran errands for the druggist. Often he waited for calls in the telephone booth in the drugstore. Since most of the people in the neighborhood didn't own phones, they were happy that the druggist provided this service. When a call came through, Abel would rush to find the person who was wanted. Most people gave Abel a penny, but once a man had dropped a nickel in Abel's hand.

When he had free time, Abel helped out in the bakery and the coffee shop.

When customers flooded in, Annie would complain, "Why can't Abel stay here when he's needed?"

"Will you pay me?" Abel would reply.

"*Pay*? My own brother?"

So, ignoring his sister's angry expression, Abel ran

off to Pincher's Grocery each morning after breakfast.

Mr. Pincher's name suited him so well, it was as if he had grown up trying to make it a good fit. He wore rimless glasses pinched onto his thin nose. Long pinched lines made deep half circles around his tight mouth. He was tall and thin, and looked as though a summer breeze could blow him away. But he was, in fact, quite strong.

Abel always arrived promptly at Pincher's — seven-thirty A.M. on the dot, for Pincher deducted from Abel's three dollars a week if he was late. Further, he expected Abel to keep busy every moment. Abel stocked shelves, swept the floor and the sidewalk, took out the garbage, helped women carry their bundles home (he sometimes got a penny tip!), and, of course, set up the fruit and produce stands on each side of the grocery store door.

Abel had just set up the stands when he heard his name called. He turned with a groan.

It was Hilda Harbinger, dark-haired, dark-eyed, tall as Abel, though she was a year younger, and known in school as The Brain, and on the block as The Pain.

"I'm busy, Hilda," Abel told her.

She paid no attention. "Listen, Abel. I've got a tremendous idea."

Abel shrugged, disappeared into the store, and staggered out again with a huge burlap sack filled with oranges.

ORANGES
24¢/lb

"Hilda," he said, over his shoulder, "I don't have time to talk. Can't you see I'm busy?"

"I'll help," she offered, as he ripped open the sack. "That way you'll get done in half the time."

"Mr. Pincher doesn't like you to help."

"Mr. Pincher doesn't like me, you mean. But that's okay, Abel. He doesn't want to get into an argument with my father."

The Harbingers lived in the apartment over Pincher's store. Harry Harbinger was a matchmaker, a widower, and a lion who roared at anyone who said a cross word about his daughter. He was a lamb to his eleven-year-old Hilda, who ran the house and her father with an iron hand.

Mr. Pincher came to the doorway, stared at Hilda, started to speak, bit his lip, and turned back into the store.

Abel had begun to pyramid the oranges as they came from the sack. Hilda, however, carefully examined each orange, and set several aside.

"Don't *do* that," Abel growled. "You want to lose me my job?"

"But these oranges are spoiled," Hilda protested.

"They aren't our oranges," Abel pointed out. "I'm just paid to stack them, not pass judgment, okay?"

Abel knew Mr. Pincher never permitted a customer to hand-pick the fruit or vegetables. So did Hilda. She bristled.

"He'll just throw the rotten ones in with the good ones."

Abel nodded. Mr. Pincher had explained the practice to Abel when Abel had questioned it. "Who am I? A millionaire? The way I have to buy them, that's the way my customers have to. I get rotten oranges. They get rotten oranges. I'm not in business for my health."

Mr. Pincher could browbeat his customers, but never Hilda. She simply examined each orange when she shopped for herself and her father. She tossed aside any orange that wasn't up to her measured eye and helped herself to replacements.

Mr. Pincher swore. Mr. Pincher raged. Mr. Pincher complained to Mr. Harbinger. Hilda remained calm.

"It's my money," she insisted. "I want what I pay for."

Mr. Pincher had to give in. He didn't want a repetition of the time Hilda made up a sandwich board sign and paced up and down in front of the store. On the sign, on both sides, Hilda had printed in big, bold letters: MR. PINCHER CHEATS!!! WATCH HIM!!!!

When Mr. Pincher complained to Hilda's father, Mr. Harbinger laughed. "Who pays attention to what a child does? Leave her alone, and she'll get tired of it."

But Hilda didn't get tired. Mr. Pincher did. He finally settled the matter by talking to Abel.

"Either she stops or you're fired."

"Wait a minute," Abel protested. "That's not fair."

"So what's fair in this world?" Mr. Pincher shrugged and went back into the store. Looking out the window, Mr. Pincher nodded and smiled when Hilda's angry face turned toward him and she angrily dropped the sign.

This morning Hilda was on fire with a solution to Abel's problem about his sister.

"Listen, Abel, I spoke to my father — "

Abel interrupted to say, "I know. I know. My grandmother spoke to him. My sister Annie spoke to him. Bruce spoke to him. So did I. Big deal. He refuses to help us."

"Will you just for once *listen*? Of course he refused. He had to. My father only takes clients who *want* to get married. Your sister Ruth — "

"I don't want to hear about my sister — "

"My father says — "

"I've heard it a million times. Your father says you can lead a horse to water, but you can't make him drink."

Hilda nodded. That was one of her father's favorite phrases.

"I made a deal with him." Hilda had to stop and wait while Abel went into the store and brought out the bananas.

"Abel," she fumed. "Can't you stop for a single

minute? Mr. Pincher has customers now. He won't notice."

Abel turned, folded his arms, tilted his head to one side, and waited.

"I talked my father into letting me go through his list of clients."

"So?"

"So this afternoon, if you're not working anywhere, we can go through his files and pick out some really good prospects."

Abel eyed her with suspicion. "What's in it for you?"

"You think I want something for myself?" Hilda tried to appear surprised at the notion.

"Hilda. This is Abel, okay? You never do anything without figuring all the angles. So I want to know. What's in it for you?"

Hilda was dying to tell him anyway. She had to share this with him or explode.

"The deal is, if we find someone for your sister Ruth, my father will send me to a summer camp for two weeks next year."

"Why?" Abel asked.

"Why?" she repeated. "What do you mean, why?"

"What's in it for your father? Why should he care?"

"You're impossible, you know that? Just plain impossible!"

Abel waited. He nodded when Hilda said, "Well, if

we find a husband for Ruth from among his clients, my father will make a good commission. Anyway, he likes Grandma Birdie. He wants to see her happy. Is that bad?"

"And it will make you happy, right? Let me guess. This camp, it has horses?"

Hilda placed her hands across her chest, closed her eyes, and sighed, "*Horses*!"

Everyone on the block knew of Hilda's passion for horses. It was no secret that she rose every morning at five to tiptoe down the steps and race to meet the milkman at the corner. He had a weary, uncomplaining horse who clip-clopped his way up and down the streets with no instruction from his owner. As the milkman swung down from his wagon, the bottles clinking in his metal carrier, the horse moved slowly on to the next stop and waited.

Hilda always greeted him lovingly. She patted and stroked and murmured. The horse would turn his head to study her and accept gratefully any small treat — an apple, a carrot, a lump of sugar.

"Isn't he beautiful?" Hilda sighed each day, as if she had just made a new discovery.

"If you say so," the milkman answered with indifference.

One morning, seeing how love flowed from Hilda, and how she yearned up at the horse, he asked, "Want to sit on him, just to find out what it feels like?"

Hilda's glowing look was like the sun breaking through on a dismal day.

The milkman swung her up. "You don't have to do anything but hold on. He knows the way."

After that, Hilda rode the horse every morning for blocks and blocks. She never minded the long walk home.

Abel had seen Hilda's room. It was papered with pictures torn out of magazines and newspapers — horses galloping, grazing, dancing, peering over fences, romping in meadows with their colts.

Abel gave the pictures only a passing glance. What Abel saw was the room itself. It wasn't large; the furniture was second-hand and ugly. But this whole space belonged to Hilda. She was eleven, but she had her own room.

Just the same, staring at Hilda now, here in front of Pincher's Grocery, Abel felt somewhat sorry for her. He knew what it was like to long for the impossible. But he couldn't waste time talking; he had a job to do. He went into the store and brought out a basket of tomatoes.

"So what do you say?" Hilda asked.

Abel shrugged. "It won't work."

"How do you know?" Hilda demanded, as she sorted out the over-ripe tomatoes and placed them to one side.

"Because Ruth isn't interested, that's why."

"But listen, Abel. You know why she isn't interested?"

Abel didn't reply. He knew Hilda would answer her own question.

"Because no one has ever actually brought somebody into the house to meet her. Have they?"

Abel stopped piling the tomatoes to stare at her. She was right. Ruth had always said with such determination that she wasn't interested, no one had ever brought a suitor to the house.

Hope began to nudge its way into his mind.

"You think . . ." he began cautiously. "I mean if we could . . ."

Hilda's smile was triumphant. "If we bring the right person, she could fall in love. It could happen. Then Ruth would want to get married."

Ruth? Fall in love? It was hard to accept the idea. Still, what if . . . just suppose that . . . *love*. Annie and Bruce were in love. When you were in love, you couldn't wait to get married.

Abel stared at Hilda with awe. "You're a genius," he whispered.

He looked down at the tomato in his hand. Tomatoes had once been called love apples. When he and Hilda found a man to invite to meet Ruth, he would put a big bowl of love apples on the table. Maybe it would work as a charm.

"So do you want to come to my house this afternoon? Around twelve-thirty? We can't get started too soon," Hilda insisted.

"Do I? Wild horses wouldn't keep me away."

Hilda laughed.

"Wild horses?" she repeated. "Is that an omen, or what?"

Neither one minded when Mr. Pincher appeared in the doorway suddenly and shouted for Hilda to go away and let Abel get on with his work.

Love, Abel thought, as he arranged a row of cabbages. Why not? Didn't Mr. Harbinger always say that it was love that made the world go round?

3

It's Kismet

Abel went straight home from the grocery store at twelve o'clock. He prepared what he called a "no-nonsense" sandwich. It piled up in layers — the bottom part of a large, seeded roll, then a generous spread of cream cheese, thickly covered with sliced onions, and overlaid with a slab of sardines drowning in mustard. Hearty pieces of tomato teetered on top. Then Abel took the top part of the roll and squashed it all down. Getting his mouth around the sandwich was a challenge. Abel pulled his mouth open until his skin stretched tight, bit, dripped, and licked the fallout.

Grandma Birdie thought it was all right for Abel to have coffee, but he preferred chocolate milk.

When he was finished eating, he cleaned up. Grandma Birdie had a rule about that, too. Then, at last, he was ready to face Hilda.

He found her in the kitchen of her apartment, with some of her father's files.

"I think we have some really good prospects here," she said. "Wait until you . . ."

Abel thought Hilda was taking over what should be his territory. After all, Ruth was his sister. He should be the one to make the decisions.

Hilda was surprised, and a little upset as well. "Hey! This was my idea, remember?" Then she added quickly, "We both have a lot to gain, Abel. It means as much to me as it does to you, even though Ruth is your family and not mine."

"Okay." Abel could see Hilda's point. "You're right. What have you found so far?"

When he leaned over Hilda, she moved back in a hurry. "Whew! You've been eating onions again!"

"Sure I have. It's brain food," he explained.

Hilda shook her head and rolled her eyes upward. "Don't you know anything? *Fish* is brain food. I eat lots of fish. That's why I'm a brain. Onions," she told him, "just clean your blood, that's all."

Abel was irritated. "Great. So you're the brain and I've got clean blood. Can we get on with this?"

Hilda said in a soothing voice, "Sure. Listen. I'll take half the papers, and you take the other half. When we come across a real hot prospect, we'll give a holler. Okay?"

They began to read Mr. Harbinger's notes, sometimes reading aloud little tidbits of information.

"Abel, listen to this. This guy says he's handsome, reliable, a swell dancer, and doesn't object to marrying for money." Hilda grinned.

"I have a better one," Abel replied. "This one says he's forty years old, is a neat dresser, has his own teeth, never eats meat, and is looking for a wife who doesn't talk too much."

They continued to read. At last, Abel, who was tired and discouraged, said, "We're wasting our time. Ruth wouldn't look at any one of these guys."

Hilda's quick temper made her reply, "She wouldn't look at *them*? Maybe it's the other way around. Maybe they wouldn't look at her."

Abel's lips tightened with anger. "What do you know about Ruth, anyway?" he demanded. "My sister Ruth is smart. She's probably the smartest sister in Brooklyn, maybe in all of New York. She's not only smart," he went on, warming up to his sister's good points, "she's a kind, caring person. Why else did she become a doctor? And she really listens to you when you talk to her. She's pretty and she's fun, and she loves us — "

Hilda held up her hand. "Hey, whoa! I'm sorry. Honest, Abel, I really am. I like Ruth. You know that."

"You have to admit this is a peculiar bunch of prospects," Abel insisted.

"Okay, you're right. They're peculiar. But I'm not giving up."

She dug into the next file, frowning, then shrieked with joy. "Abel! Here's one. And another one. And *another* one. Three in a row. And you were ready to give up."

Abel wasn't persuaded. "Remember," he warned. "We don't want just anybody. After all, Ruth *is* a doctor. She's not just some ordinary person."

Hilda waved a sheet in front of him. "You'll die when you hear this, Abel. You'll just die."

Abel sat back in his chair, folded his arms, and waited impatiently to die.

" 'I am thirty-five years old, a bank manager . . .' " Hilda broke off to repeat in awe. "A *bank* manager! 'I am intelligent, well read, handsome, a home owner, a catch for a young woman who can meet my standards. I am interested in marrying at once, and want a large family.' "

"He sure thinks a lot of himself, doesn't he?"

"Of course he does, dummy. He's a *bank* manager. How many bank managers do you know?"

"How would I know a bank manager?" Abel asked reasonably.

"Maybe you think a bank manager isn't good enough for a doctor?" Hilda went on.

"I didn't say that . . ."

"You better not, Abel Stoner. Now listen, here's what we're going to do."

Abel sighed. *There she goes*, he told himself. *Tak-*

ing over as though she owns the world.

Hilda paid no attention. She was busy scribbling the prospective suitor's name and address. She read it aloud as she did so. "Henry Gates, 444 Park Crescent Row. We'll have to take the trolley, Abel. This must be right near Prospect Park."

"Wait a minute. Not so fast," Abel roared. "You said you had three good prospects. What about the others?"

"You still want to hear about them?" Hilda couldn't believe it. "After we just discovered the perfect husband for Ruth?"

When Abel insisted, she began to read the other names. "Harold Trumpet. High school teacher." She paused. "Abel! A high school teacher. And he teaches *math*." Hilda was visibly impressed.

She and Abel knew that teachers were not your everyday mortals. Teachers were . . . they were . . . she searched for a word in her mind — they were *teachers*! And Harold Trumpet had to be some kind of superteacher to teach math.

Abel wriggled uncomfortably. "I don't know. I don't think I'd want a teacher to be my brother-in-law."

"It would be awfully hard," Hilda admitted. "You'd always have to be on your best behavior whenever he was around. But I bet your Grandma Birdie would love it."

Abel nodded. He knew exactly how his grandmother would feel. She'd be bursting with pride. He could almost hear her say, "My Ruth, the doctor, is married to a schoolteacher. A *high* school teacher."

Grandma Birdie would be the envy of everyone in the neighborhood. She'd walk around, head high, as if she'd just been made queen of the universe.

On the other hand, Abel reflected, Grandma Birdie would probably also be scared all the time, afraid that her speech wouldn't be refined and proper. A teacher would find fault with the way she dressed, or ate, or whatever.

Abel had another thought. How would Annie react? Would she be jealous because Ruth would marry well, while Annie planned to marry a butcher's son?

Hilda began to read on. "Harold Trumpet. High school teacher. Tall, dark, slender. Fine personality. Age thirty. Am studying for my Ph. D." Hilda stopped reading abruptly. She was a brain, but she had no idea what a Ph. D. was.

Abel was equally puzzled. "What's that?"

Hilda shrugged. "I can't explain it to you," she said, pretending to be knowledgeable. "It's something very special. Wow! He's almost better than a bank manager. What do you think, Abel?"

"Does he say anything else?"

"Yes. He wants a well-educated girl."

"Like Ruth!" Abel cried.

"Who must have a warm personality," Hilda continued. "Uh-oh. That could be a problem."

"What do you mean, uh-oh?" Abel flared. "Ruth may not show it with strangers, but she has a very warm personality. People who don't know her think she's cold because she's quiet."

Hilda rushed to soothe Abel's anger. "Maybe she does have a warm personality when she's with people she really and truly likes. It's just that she's not bubbly, like Annie. You have to admit, Abel, that even at home, Ruth doesn't talk very much."

Abel was insulted. "You think, because she's quiet, she doesn't like us? Her own family?"

"That's different," Hilda explained. "You're just yourself with your own family. You don't have to be interesting, or anything."

Abel understood. Didn't Annie walk around in a sloppy housecoat, with her hair uncombed? But when she went down to work in the store, or waited for Bruce, she became transformed.

"Okay," Abel agreed. "We can give him a try. Now read about the next one."

"Abel! What more do we need? We have the very best two right here."

"Read." Abel's voice was frosty.

"Boys," Hilda muttered under her breath. "What

do they know? George Fox," she began. "Manufacturer. Owns the factory. Age sixty — "

"Sixty?" Abel repeated. "Are you out of your mind? He's old enough to be Ruth's grandfather."

Hilda ignored him. "He's rich," she pointed out. "He says he's a widower, with two grown children and four grandchildren —"

Abel held up his hand, like a policeman stopping traffic in every direction. "Forget it, Hilda."

"I'm not finished. He's prepared to give the woman who marries him every comfort. Every comfort," she repeated emphatically. "Do you know what that means? Ruth would never have to work a day in her life if she didn't feel like it." Before Abel could interrupt her again, she added, "He says his only requirement is that his future wife be compatible."

Abel stared at her. "Compatible? What does that mean, compatible?"

Hilda answered with some impatience. "I guess he wants somebody he can get along with." She bit her lip. "You think Ruth could learn to be compatible?"

"Don't start in with that stuff about Ruth again," Abel warned.

"Which one shall we interview first?" Hilda sprang up, ready to go.

"We can't go now. Maybe nobody will be home in the afternoon. Let's wait until after supper."

GEORGE FOX:
MANUFACTURER
OWNS THE FACTORY
AGE: 60
WIDOWER, TWO GROWN CHILDREN
HIGH SCHOOL
AGE: 30
STUDYING

"Then eat it fast," Hilda advised. "We have no time to waste."

Hilda looked off into space.

Horses, Abel told himself. *She's thinking about horses again.*

Abel picked up the three sheets in his right hand, then shifted them back and forth. *How will we choose*? he wondered.

"You can't decide, right? Put them face down on the table," Hilda instructed. "Mix them up. Then pick one. After all," she added generously, "she is your sister."

Abel slid the papers around and around. Then he took a deep breath, closed his eyes, and chose one of the sheets at random.

"Let me see," Hilda shouted. Then she laughed with delight.

"Abel. You picked the bank manager. It's Kismet. Fate," she explained, sure that Abel had never heard the word.

"Kismet," he repeated softly.

It was meant to be. The bank manager. How could Ruth resist?

4

Big Families Are Wonderful

Abel was glad of any excuse to ride a trolley. He liked summertime trips best, for then the trolley was open on both sides.

Gentle breezes touched his face; the late sunlight dappled in and out as the trolley rode its tracks east and then north. He enjoyed watching the passing scene.

"I wish I could go around the world on a trolley," he murmured.

"Sure," said practical Hilda. "Cross the ocean and everything on a trolley. You need to have your head examined, Abel."

"You have no imagination," he complained, but he felt too relaxed to get into an argument. He liked to dream, that's all. Summer days and evenings were made for dreaming, weren't they?

Hilda sprang to her feet, shouting, "Come on, Abel. This is where we get off."

Abel left the trolley reluctantly. As they walked, Abel asked, "Did you tell your father where we were going?"

She gave him a sidelong glance. "Not exactly. I just told him I was going for a walk to the playground with you. Did you tell your grandmother?"

"She was busy in the store. I didn't want to bother her."

Hilda laughed. "Sure."

Abel looked at his street map. The area near the park seemed to run off in every direction. He stopped to study it, then put his finger down hard. "Here it is. Crescent Park Row." He glanced up at the street sign. "It must be a couple of blocks more."

Hilda marched smartly at his side until they reached the house in which the bank manager lived. She paused, uncertain, to read the name printed under the doorbell.

"The Gates Residence," she read aloud.

The Gates Residence? It was a nice house, or so it seemed from the outside. But it was only a house. Why did the bank manager have to call it a residence?

"I've never been in a residence," Hilda said uneasily. She seemed ready now to turn away and leave.

"No, you don't." Abel grabbed her arm and held on. "It was your idea. Well, let's get it over with. He won't bite," he added bravely.

He pushed the bell hard with his forefinger and waited with a determined look.

After a couple of minutes, the door swung open. A tall woman, with iron gray hair and steel blue eyes, regarded them. Around her neck she wore a silver chain from which a pair of glasses dangled.

"Yes?" she asked, in a cold, unfriendly voice. "What are you children doing, ringing this bell? Are you selling something? Whatever it is, I'm not interested."

Hilda whispered to Abel, "He won't bite? I bet *she* does."

"What's that? Speak up," the woman commanded sharply.

"We came to see Mr. Henry Gates. Is he home?" Abel asked.

"Who wants him? Did someone send you with a message? You can give it to me." She held out her hand as if she expected a note to be placed there.

"It's personal," Hilda told her.

"I'm his mother. Is that personal enough for you, young lady?"

Abel began to back off, but Hilda stood her ground. They had a right to be here, hadn't they? Weren't they here on legitimate business?

"Mr. Gates asked my father . . . my father is the matchmaker. Mr. Harbinger? Mr. Gates wants my father to find a wife for him."

"Oh." The woman glared at Hilda, as if the whole idea of her son going to a matchmaker was Hilda's fault. "Well, he isn't here. He's at a meeting."

"Will you tell him he's invited for Sunday supper — this Sunday — to meet a very nice prospect? Six o'clock Sunday? At this address?" Hilda handed the woman a small slip of paper with the information carefully written out in clear, block letters.

The woman snatched it, even as she said, in a voice that sounded as if she had bitten into a sour apple, "I don't approve of this at all. But I'll tell him."

"She's like the king who wanted to kill the messenger for bringing him bad news," Abel commented, as they walked away. "I bet she doesn't even want him to get married."

"Of course she doesn't. Mothers never want their sons to get married, only their daughters," Hilda said with a knowing air.

Before Abel had a chance to reply, Hilda rushed on, "Because mothers never think any girl is good enough for their sons, that's why."

Abel stopped in midstep, swung around, and demanded, "You mean Grandma Birdie would like Ruth to get married? And Annie? But not me?"

"Wait and see," was Hilda's response. "I'm right. I'm always right."

Abel brooded on the way home. How come Hilda

always thought she knew the answer to everything? She'd better be careful. She could get to be too smart. Then who would want to marry *her*?

When they reached their street, Abel was struck with a sudden thought. He'd never even told Grandma his plans. Suppose she didn't want a guest for supper Sunday night.

"Suppose Grandma gets mad at me," Abel said aloud.

Hilda's look was one of utter disbelief.

"Not want to have a prospective husband come for supper? She'll welcome him with hugs and kisses. She'll roll out the welcome mat. She'll — "

"Okay. Okay," Abel interrupted. "I get the idea."

Hilda proved to be only half right. It was true that Grandma Birdie was delighted. She prepared a feast, with every one of her specialties spread out on the table. She didn't even object when Abel placed a bowl of large, red-ripe tomatoes in the center of the table, especially when he told her it was for good luck. Good luck was what she prayed for this evening.

"It's a feast for royalty," Grandma Birdie crowed, then put her hand to her mouth and looked worried. "But where is Ruth?"

Where *was* Ruth? Abel wondered.

"Look at that." Grandma Birdie sounded both anxious and irritated. "Everybody is here. Annie and Bruce. You and me. Hilda — "

Abel shot Hilda a dark glance. "Who asked her, anyway?"

"She invited herself. Poor child. When does she get a chance to eat a real, homemade meal?"

Often, Abel was tempted to say. Hilda was no stranger at mealtimes.

Hilda winked at him. Well, Abel decided, maybe she had a right to be present after all, since finding Henry Gates and the others was her idea in the first place.

When the bell rang, Abel raced to the door, but Hilda beat him to it. She flung it open and stared wide-eyed. The man standing in the doorway was tall; he was handsome. His thick hair was black and swept up in waves away from his high forehead. His eyes were large and brightly black, and seemed to Abel to bore right through him. His dark mustache curled around his lips into a pointed, carefully shaped beard.

"This is the Stoner residence?" he asked.

Abel was surprised. His apartment was a residence? He tested the word in his mind. *Residence*. He liked it, and glared at Hilda when she giggled.

"Please come in," Abel said.

Mr. Gates shook hands with Bruce, smiled at Annie,

and complimented Grandma Birdie on what she was wearing.

Grandma Birdie bloomed. She had put on her best silk dress, along with the large cameo pin she had inherited from her mother. She wore it only at weddings, but this dinner might lead to one, she told Abel, as she pinned it on.

"He has such beautiful manners," Grandma Birdie whispered to Annie, and in the same breath asked, "So where is Ruth, tell me?"

As if Grandma Birdie had wished her in, Ruth came out of her bedroom. Grandma Birdie beamed. Ruth looked beautiful. Her dress was new and most becoming. It flattered her figure and made her seem taller. She had even put on high-heeled shoes, a triple-strand pearl necklace, and tiny pearl earrings.

"I'd like you to meet my granddaughter Ruth. This is our honored guest, Mr. Gates. The bank manager," she added, with emphasis.

Mr. Gates smiled, said it was his pleasure, pulled out a chair for Ruth, then sat down beside her.

Between passing dishes, praising the food, and eating heartily, Henry Gates managed to have a conversation with Ruth. Everyone listened hard, especially Grandma Birdie.

"I must say you're a beautiful young woman," he began.

Grandma Birdie looked triumphant. Hilda gave Abel a smug smile.

"My father can make reservations at camp for me," she whispered to Abel.

"I do hope we can have a meeting of the minds," Henry Gates went on. "I think — "

"Excuse me," Bruce interrupted. "You're a good-looking man. You have a fine job. How come you want a matchmaker to find a wife for you?"

Everyone seemed embarrassed by Bruce's blunt question. But Mr. Gates was not embarrassed.

"It's simple, really," he explained. "I'm not very good at dating. I get nervous and tongue-tied — "

Grandma Birdie couldn't help interrupting. "But you're a bank manager," she cried. "You talk to people all day long."

"That's different. That's business. Dating is something else. I can't help it. I'm shy."

Abel stared. This tall, good-looking man, this bank manager, was shy? What a ridiculous thing for him to say. Kids could be shy — Abel sometimes felt that way in the presence of strangers — but a shy grown-up? How was that possible?

He was about to ask, changed his mind, and said instead, "Is that why you went to a matchmaker?"

"Exactly. I told Mr. Harbinger the kind of girl I'm looking for. Matchmakers are good at what they do. I knew he would find the right person for me sooner or later — " he paused to smile at Ruth — "and now it seems as if he's found her."

"How come you're not shy now?" Abel wanted to know.

"Abel." Grandma Birdie frowned at him and would have scolded him for asking too many questions, but Henry Gates held up his hand.

"Please. The boy wants an explanation. That's fine with me. I'm not shy now," he told Abel, "because this is not a date. Understand? I know what I want. Your sister knows what she wants."

He sat back and beamed at everyone. Then he sighed.

"You can't imagine how nervous I was on the way over, the kind of thoughts that ran through my mind. Thank goodness that's over with. Now all it will take is for Ruth to say yes, and — "

"But you don't know anything about me," Ruth protested. "You don't know what I like, what I don't like, what I do . . ."

He patted her hand. "Listen, Ruth. It will be all right. I'll have to get used to you. You'll have to get used to me. But we will. Don't worry. I'm sure we're both sensible, and can work out any little problems that might come up."

Grandma Birdie agreed with him. She nodded.

"You're one hundred percent right."

Abel could tell his grandmother was already visualizing Ruth in her wedding gown, and planning the special wedding cake she would bake for this wonderful occasion.

Hilda decided at this point to be helpful.

"Ruth is no ordinary person, Mr. Gates," she told him. "She's a doctor."

"A doctor?" He was surprised. "I've never met a woman doctor before."

"Do you have a problem with that?" Bruce demanded.

Annie frowned at him, but Bruce didn't care. He admired Ruth, and he wanted everyone else to admire her as well.

Henry Gates was lost in thought for a moment. "The idea takes getting used to," he said. Then he smiled. "Still, it would be very impressive to say 'my wife, the doctor.' Yes sir. Very impressive." He turned to Ruth and placed his hand over hers. "Do you like children?"

"Yes, of course," she told him, "but — "

Before she could finish, he rushed on. "I'm an only child. It's awful to be an only child. Big families have so much going for them. Just think about holidays, for example. Brothers and sisters, uncles and aunts, cousins, grandparents, and the children! All breaking bread together. I've never experienced anything like that. My mother and I are alone. She's an only child, too."

Ruth was touched. But again he spoke before she could. "What I want, more than anything in this world, is a house full of children. And then, grandchildren. I can't wait to be a grandfather." His eyes became dreamy. "I want us to have family reunions — "

"And you should have all that," Ruth put in quickly. "But not with me. I'm sorry, Henry. I'm really and truly sorry. I've worked very hard to become a doctor. It hasn't been easy. I'm not ready to give it up now for marriage and a family, at least not for a few years yet."

Grandma Birdie shook her head, as if to say, "How can she turn down such a fine man?"

Annie and Bruce moved a little closer to one another. Abel could tell they felt sorry for Henry Gates.

Hilda kicked Abel under the table. "There goes camp," she whispered angrily.

Camp? Abel thought. What was camp compared with his loss?

Henry Gates rose. "I think we could have been happy." He sent Ruth a wistful glance. "Well, I'd better be going. I'm sorry it didn't work out. I wish you success in your career, Ruth."

Ruth sprang up and kissed him on the cheek.

"Don't give up," she encouraged him. "Someone is out there for you. I'm sure of it. Let me know when you find her, will you?"

He promised, though he seemed doubtful.

After he was gone, no one seemed in the mood for conversation. Bruce and Annie decided to go to the movies. Grandma Birdie looked discouraged, then she shrugged.

"I guess it wasn't meant to be. This time," she added, not one to give up.

Ruth dropped a kiss on her grandmother's head. "I have to look over some records in my office. I'll be back in a little while."

When the door closed behind her, Grandma Birdie said, "So I suppose nobody wants a napoleon now, right?"

"Wrong!" Hilda shouted. She could eat napoleons at any time of day or night. That's what she told Grandma Birdie as soon as she demolished the first one, and she asked for another.

Abel pushed his napoleon aside.

With her spoon halfway to her mouth, Hilda consoled him. "Never mind, Abel. Don't forget we still have two more lively prospects."

Abel didn't answer. Getting his own room suddenly seemed a forlorn hope.

5

He's Not the Only Pebble on the Beach

Grandma Birdie glanced down at her dress and smoothed away a tiny crumb. "I'm going to change," she announced. "I don't want anything to happen to my best silk dress."

Abel, upset and angry, took out his frustration on his grandmother. "Why do you keep calling it your best silk dress?" he demanded. "It's the *only* silk dress you have."

She shrugged. "So? If it's the only, then it has to be the best. I'll change, then I'll come back and clear everything away."

"No," Abel told her, sorry now that he had hurt her feelings. "You go ahead, Grandma. I'll take care of everything."

"And I'll help." Hilda began to remove the platters on which there were still some untouched portions of food. "I'll put this stuff in the icebox."

In winter, Grandma Birdie stored food in a tin box

attached to the ledge outside the kitchen window. In warm weather, she bought large blocks of ice from the iceman.

Abel had always been fascinated by the iceman, a burly, unsmiling individual who slung a burlap sack over one shoulder, hoisted an enormous chunk of ice atop the sack, then carried it upstairs to flip it into the top part of the icebox.

Grandma, who often paid as much as twenty cents for the ice, carefully wrapped newspapers around it, to make it last longer. It was Abel's job to empty the container under the icebox when it filled up with water.

Sometimes Abel and Hilda, and the other children in the neighborhood, chased after the ice truck. Then, while the iceman made his deliveries, they sneaked bits of ice to suck on, as a special treat.

When his grandmother came back into the room, wearing a sensible house dress, she said, "I'll just run down to the store and talk to Himmel."

As soon as she left, Hilda said, "I might as well go home."

She was tired of Abel's moody silence as he slammed dishes back into the cabinets, and silverware into a drawer.

"Who's stopping you?" was his immediate response. "You and your big idea," he added, under his breath.

Hilda's hearing was keen. "You can be a real swift

pain in the neck, you know that, Abel? One little setback and you're ready to call it quits."

He turned so she could receive the full force of his glare.

"You don't get it, do you? We're wasting our time. Ruth is as stubborn as Grandma, and that is grade-A stubborn. A mule could take lessons from both of them."

"What about love?" Hilda wanted to know.

Abel shook his head in disbelief.

"Love?" he echoed. "*Love*?"

"It could happen." Hilda searched her mind for some examples. "What about Bruce and Annie? What about . . . let me think . . . what about Caesar and Cleopatra?"

"They didn't live in Brooklyn," Abel replied. "Anyway, Ruth isn't a Cleopatra, and if she was, where would we find a Caesar?"

"There's no talking to you when you're like this," she flared, but continued anyway. "So Henry Gates wasn't Mr. Right. He's not the only pebble on the beach."

Abel wished Hilda wouldn't quote her father's favorite expressions.

"Pebbles," he repeated. "How many pebbles do we have? Three," he told her, before she could reply. "A big three. And one of the pebbles is back on the beach. I still say we should forget the whole thing."

"And I think you have rocks in your head." Hilda scowled. "Tell me you changed your mind and don't want your own room anymore — "

"Just leave me alone, okay, Hilda? Just go home and leave me alone."

Hilda went on as if he hadn't spoken. "Of course you do. And I want to go to summer camp. So we're not giving up, get me?" She ignored his wince as her finger jabbed his side.

"Will you stop poking me?" he yelled. "Okay. Okay. I'll give it one more chance. Which one shall we try next, then?"

"The schoolteacher," Hilda decided. "You know how Grandma Birdie feels about teachers."

Abel nodded. Even Ruth, he thought, would have to like a teacher. He would be a professional person, after all. Ruth could respect and admire another professional.

"We can make plans tomorrow. After I'm through working at Pincher's. And don't come hanging around talking to me," he warned. "Pincher doesn't like it. He said — "

"I don't care what he said." Hilda had fire in her eyes. "He can't push me around. I live over the store. They're my sidewalks, too. Anyway, sidewalks belong to everybody. They're public property."

She had told that to Mr. Pincher, whose cold response was, "Young lady, when you pay taxes, come back and talk to me about public property." He had then favored Abel with a furious glance. Abel could almost see the words "you're fired" trembling on his lips.

Abel asked now, as he often did, "What's the matter with you, Hilda? Why can't you act like a girl?"

"I *am* acting like a girl. What do you think girls have, sawdust instead of brains?"

Abel shook his head. Hilda was hopeless. He didn't know anyone else who stood up for her rights with such vigor.

The room was wonderfully quiet after Hilda left. Abel sank down on the couch, grateful to be alone with his thoughts. One couldn't do much thinking with Hilda around — explosive, demanding Hilda.

He began to relive the evening. Henry Gates had been a pleasant surprise, especially after the meeting with his mother, the dragon lady. Abel had liked Henry Gates and had been sorry for him. How sad he made it seem to be an only child.

"I'm lucky," Abel said aloud. "I have Grandma Birdie, and Annie, and Ruth. And I have Bruce."

The mention of Bruce reminded Abel that he wanted to practice the Morse code. This was an ideal time to do it. When the others were present, they became impatient with his constant tapping.

He jumped up and went to the table. With a pencil, he went through the entire alphabet. It was much easier now. Constant practice did make a difference.

"Teach me the Morse code," Hilda had demanded once. But Abel had refused. There had to be something he could do that Hilda couldn't.

"I'll teach myself," she had threatened.

She probably would, too. Abel grinned. Hilda seemed to be able to do anything she wanted, if she wanted it hard enough.

"Just like Ruth," Abel said aloud, as he sometimes did when he was alone.

He wondered why some people thought it was wrong for a woman to be ambitious, but right for a man. When he grew up and married, he'd let his wife do what she wished. If she was like Ruth, he would encourage her and help her all he could.

Too bad Ruth couldn't meet someone like Bruce. Bruce thought the world of Ruth. He didn't feel she was a threat to him because she was a doctor, and he was only the son of a butcher.

Bruce. He was lucky, too. His mother and father thought the sun rose and set just for Bruce. If Bruce wanted the world with a string around it, his parents would try to give it to him. Though ball games bored Mr. Jonas, he took Bruce to Ebbetts Field every chance he could. They went to Prospect Park so Bruce could row on the lake, though Mr. Jonas claimed he got seasick just watching water flow into the bathtub. He bought his son a bike, then he and Mrs. Jonas worried as soon as Bruce was out of sight.

Abel's musing was interrupted by the sound of a key in the lock. Good. Bruce and Annie had come home early. Noticing Abel's surprise, Bruce explained, "The movie was boring."

Boring? How could any movie be boring? Abel always sat through a movie twice, in case he missed something during the first showing.

"Have you been working on the code?" Bruce asked.

Abel nodded. "Bruce, can I ask you something?"

Bruce winked at Annie. "If this is boy talk, maybe Annie should scram out of here."

Annie laughed. "I'm on my way. I want to see what Grandma and Himmel are up to anyway."

With a wave of her hand, she left the room to go downstairs.

"I just wanted to know. You're an only child. Is that the way you feel, like Mr. Gates? About being an only child?"

"No. I don't know about him, but I was never lonely. I always had lots of friends. I still do."

Abel nodded. "Especially your ham friends, right, Bruce?"

"Even before I became a ham. My folks always did a lot for me." He smiled. "My parents even let me help out in the store, almost before I could walk. I probably got in the way more than I helped."

Bruce went to the icebox to help himself to some milk. When he came back, he had a white mustache, since he liked to drink right from the bottle. Annie always scolded him when she caught him, so he did it only when she wasn't around.

"By the time I was five," Bruce continued, "I could name every cut of meat. I knew the difference between a pullet and a hen."

"That's not like having sisters and brothers," Abel objected.

"There were plenty of kids on the block. And there was Annie. There was always Annie."

Bruce had claimed Annie from the day their grandmother had taken Ruth, Abel, and Annie to live with her.

"Do you want a big family, like Henry Gates?" Abel wondered.

"Of course Annie and I want a family. I can't guarantee how big it will be." Bruce laughed.

"Hilda and I have two other prospects for Ruth. Hilda thinks we should invite them — one at a time," Abel added in haste. "She says Ruth could fall in love with one of them. You think we should go ahead with our plan?"

"What have you got to lose?" Bruce asked. "I say, full speed ahead."

Abel agreed. What did he have to lose?

All of a sudden, he felt better. Maybe there was still hope, after all.

6

Don't Bring a Cake

The next morning, when Abel couldn't get into the bathroom to brush his teeth, because first Ruth, then Annie, locked the door, he began to fume. What he needed was not only a room of his own, he thought, but a bathroom all for himself as well. Women! Why did he have to be outnumbered by females?

Somehow, this feeling suddenly extended to include Hilda. Hilda and her ideas. Hilda and her wonderful prospect, Henry Gates. Why had he allowed himself to be talked into this whole mess?

When he showed up at Pincher's Grocery, he glanced around warily. Good. No Hilda in sight. In fact, no Hilda all morning. It would suit Abel if he didn't see Hilda for at least a week.

On arriving home when he was through at the grocery, however, Hilda was waiting for him. She was in the kitchen, where she had just finished lunch.

"You want some lunch?" she asked.

Abel wasn't surprised to find Hilda making herself at home. He had long since gotten used to the fact that Hilda treated his family as if she were part of it. She walked in and out of the apartment as if she had every right to do so.

At first Abel had complained. Did he really need one more female in his life? Grandma Birdie was shocked.

"A child without a mother," she scolded him. "Without a family . . ."

"She has a father," Abel pointed out, and almost added, "which is more than I have."

"A father is not a whole family," Grandma Birdie informed him coldly. "Sisters are a family. A grandmother is a family. A father by himself is not a family."

Abel rolled his eyes upward. Who could argue with his grandmother's special logic? Maybe there were rules about what makes a family.

"Come back, come back, wherever you are," Hilda chanted. She never liked being excluded from Abel's thoughts. "Do you want lunch? Yes or no."

Abel regarded her with suspicion. "Why? You want something, don't you?"

"Me?" Hilda asked, with an injured air. "Just because I'm trying to be nice to you?"

"I'll make my own lunch, thank you."

Hilda watched as he took the fixings out of the icebox. "You're not going to put that stuff into your stomach." She sounded horrified.

Abel ignored her. He began with a large slice of seeded rye bread. He spread it with mustard, then with ketchup. Limburger cheese nestled on top of that, followed by several slices of onion capped by the second slice of rye.

"Limburger cheese *and* onion?" Hilda moved back out of range. "People will be walking on the other side of the street to get away from you," she cried.

Abel grinned. "Maybe you ought to go home now," he suggested, "to get away from the fumes."

Hilda stood her ground. She had something to say, and nothing — not even the combination of Limburger cheese and an onion strong enough to fell an ox — was going to stop her.

"I decided," she began, while keeping a somewhat worried eye on him, "that we should invite *two* prospects for Sunday-night supper."

Abel had been ready to bite into his sandwich. Now he stood stricken, mouth spread open as far as he could stretch it. He snapped his mouth closed so hard he could feel his jaw crack.

"*You* decided?" he roared. "*You* decided?"

"What's the matter with you?" She gave him a hostile look. "Don't you want your sister to get married anymore?"

Abel regarded his sandwich gloomily. He'd been so hungry when he came home. He was still hungry, he supposed, but somehow the sandwich didn't seem quite as appetizing. He pushed it aside.

"I suppose you have what you'd call a good reason?"

"The problem was, with this guy Gates, Ruth didn't get to have a choice. It was him or nobody, see? But if we have two prospects at the same time, she can make a comparison — "

Abel interrupted thoughtfully. "And they could be competition for each other."

"Right! Maybe if they see they're not the only pebbles — "

"Hilda," Abel warned. "If you say that one more time, I'll glue your lips together."

She ignored the threat. "So I brought paper and a pen and a bottle of ink, and we can get started with the invitations right away."

"Whoa!" Abel yelled. "What invitations?"

Hilda stared at him as if she couldn't believe that anyone could reach the age of twelve and still be so ignorant.

"Invitations," she repeated. "It's a whole lot more elegant than ringing a doorbell. That's like begging. An invitation is . . ." she searched her mind for a better word, but couldn't think of one that fit so well . . . "elegant."

"He came, didn't he? Isn't that the whole idea?"

Hilda cleared a generous space on the table, sat down, pulled a sheet of paper close, and nibbled on the tip of the pen. Then she asked, somewhat helplessly, "What shall I say?"

Abel sighed. "How should I know? I never sent anybody an invitation before. I never even received one. Why can't you just come right out and say, you want to marry my sister Ruth? Come this Sunday and — "

"You can't do that!" Hilda was aghast.

"Why not? That's what we want. That's what they want. Everybody knows what everybody wants. Why can't we just say so?"

"Never mind. I can see I have to do this myself." Hilda closed her eyes, the better to think. Soon her pen raced across the sheet.

Abel waited until she was finished.

"Can I hear the masterpiece now?" he wondered.

Hilda read it aloud as if she were reciting in school.

> Dear Mr. Trumpet:
> You are cordially invited for supper this Sunday night to meet your future bride, Ruth Belle Stoner, who is very pretty and smart and interested in meeting a nice person to marry. Supper is at six o'clock. Don't bring a cake because she lives over a bakery.

"What do you think?" she asked anxiously.

"It sounds all right to me. How are you going to sign it?"

"Oh!" Hilda hadn't thought of that.

"I'm putting down Grandma Birdie and this address. Shall I sign her name?"

"No way."

"Why? Does Grandma Birdie have a rule about that?" Hilda wanted to know.

"Of course she does. Sign somebody else's name to something they didn't write? What do you think?"

Hilda had an inspiration. She picked up the pen and swiftly wrote a name. Abel, peering over her shoulder, was shocked.

"You wrote your father's name. You can't do that," he exclaimed.

"No, I didn't. All I put down is Harbinger. That's all."

"But he'll think it's your father."

"Well, it's my name, too, isn't it? Anyway, what difference does it make? He's one of my father's clients."

Abel had to agree with Hilda. Her father's clients wanted to get married.

He watched as she rewrote the letter, careful to shape her words, trying hard not to drop blotches of ink on the page. Then she addressed an envelope.

She wrote the same letter to the third prospect, George Fox, the businessman.

"I need two two-cent stamps," she announced.

"Don't look at me," Abel told her. "I don't have any stamps. Well, don't look so surprised. What do I need with stamps? I never write to anybody."

"I have to go home now anyway. I'll put stamps on the letters and mail them." She gave Abel a broad smile. "This is it, Abel. I can tell. I have a feeling we're going to be lucky." Her eyes glowed. "You want to bet I'll be going to camp next summer?"

Horses, Abel thought. *She wants her horses, and I want my own room.*

What better reasons could there be for Ruth to get married?

7

The Unexpected Guest

"You invited a teacher to come here? To this house?" Grandma Birdie was stunned. She couldn't believe her good fortune. But she was also in a state of frenzy.

Glancing about wildly, she declared, "We'll have to turn the whole apartment upside-down."

Abel groaned. That meant an onslaught of cleaning. Everyone, of course, was pressed into service, except Ruth, who declared she might not even be present for the wonderful coming of Harold Trumpet.

Annie was ordered to wash all the woodwork. Hilda was instructed to inspect every corner of the apartment and wherever else a speck of dust might linger. Abel was charged with polishing every glass surface, including all the windows, with Grandma Birdie's special formula of ammonia and scalding water.

"I'll pass out from the fumes," Abel predicted gloomily.

"First polish, then pass out," was his grandmother's hardhearted reply.

Even the furniture was moved, and the floor underneath scrubbed.

"You think he's going to come in and look under all the furniture to see if everything is spotless?" Abel wanted to know.

"Teachers can see things we can't," his grandmother informed him. "Teachers have eyes in the back of their heads."

That was true, Abel thought. His English teacher, old Miss Maplewood, for instance, knew exactly what everyone was up to, even when she had her back to the class.

"George Michael Parry," she would say, while writing adverbs and adjectives on the blackboard, "you throw one more spitball and you'll march right down to see the principal."

Or, "Jenny Sue Block, bring that romance magazine here and throw it in the basket with the rest of the trash."

Oh, yes. Miss Maplewood had eyes in the back of her head, and they watched the class every single minute.

When all the chores had been done, Grandma Birdie gave the apartment one final, thorough inspection. Only then did she relax somewhat.

"Everything looks so beautiful, it's a shame that businessman —"

"George Fox," Hilda said.

Grandma Birdie nodded. "It's a shame he can't come this Sunday, too." Secretly, though, she was delighted. What suitor could shine in the presence of a teacher?

George Fox had written a note and had it hand delivered. He'd be away for the weekend to attend a wedding. But he would like to come the following Sunday, if that was all right.

"A wedding!" Grandma Birdie had exclaimed. "That's a good sign."

By the time Sunday suppertime rolled round, everyone was in a high state of expectation and hope. Everyone, that is, except Ruth. She was edgy and irritated.

"You had no right to invite that man to come here to meet me," she exclaimed in a rare temper tantrum.

"But he's a teacher," Abel tried to explain. "I just thought—"

"I know what you just thought, and I won't have it, Abel. Understand? I don't need a twelve-year-old boy to arrange my life for me."

Nobody could pick on Abel when his grandmother was present. She charged in. "So what did he do that's so terrible? It's not the end of the world. If you don't like the man, you just say hello and goodbye and that's it. Believe me, we won't hold a wedding the minute the teacher walks in the door."

Abel sat at the table and brooded. It was Hilda. She was the one who got him into trouble. He should never have listened to her. He regarded her with angry eyes.

Hilda sank back in her chair. Who knew that Ruth would explode this way? It wasn't fair. Ruth wasn't fair. Then she sat up straight, her eyes beaming. Suppose Ruth fell in love, wham! the minute she saw Harold Trumpet. Their eyes would meet. Ruth's hand would dart to her throat. Harold Trumpet would become rooted to the spot. Love at First sight.

Why couldn't it happen that way?

Hilda was about to confide her thoughts to Abel when the doorbell rang.

Grandma Birdie looked at the clock on the wall. It wasn't six o'clock yet. The teacher was early. Another good sign, she told herself.

"I wish Bruce was here," Ruth said.

Abel nodded. Bruce protected her, and she liked that.

Annie shrugged. "If some ham spotted Bruce's aerial on the roof and dropped in on him, Bruce will forget about being here for supper."

Hilda sped to the door. Here at last was the man

who had described himself as tall, dark, slender, with a fine personality.

"How do you do, Mr. Trumpet? Won't you come in?"

Hilda tried to sound grown-up, as though she welcomed teachers all the time. She was, in fact, awed. To meet a teacher outside the classroom felt quite odd.

As Harold Trumpet moved forward, Hilda shot a hopeful glance at Ruth. Had her hand flown to her throat? Hilda sighed. Of course not. Ruth was her usual self — calm, quiet, reserved.

Grandma Birdie came forward to greet their guest. "Welcome, Mr. Trumpet. I'd like you to meet everybody."

As Grandma Birdie pronounced each name, Harold Trumpet nodded. When she introduced Ruth, however he took her hand, gave her a warm smile, and said in a deep voice, "My pleasure."

Hilda flashed Abel a triumphant look.

Abel knew that look well. It meant Hilda was positive things would turn out the way she had planned.

"Sit. Sit," Grandma Birdie instructed, and pointed to the chair next to Ruth.

For a moment, Abel was afraid Ruth would be cold, the way she always was when she was angry. Then he felt ashamed. He knew Ruth better than that. She would never make a guest in their home feel uncomfortable.

"Tell me about yourself," Ruth said to their guest. "I understand you teach math in high school."

Harold Trumpet nodded as he helped himself to a generous portion of Grandma Birdie's stuffed cabbage, carefully spooning gravy and raisins onto his dish. He took one bite, then another.

"Marvelous," he said. "You made this?" he asked Ruth.

She laughed. "I'm a terrible cook. You're sampling my grandmother's specialty."

Mr. Trumpet stopped eating long enough to tell Ruth, "I don't plan to teach in high school too much longer."

Grandma Birdie's spoon clattered to her dish.

"You don't want to be a teacher anymore?"

It was as if a disaster had been announced.

Harold Trumpet laughed. "You sounded just like my mother then. Of course I still want to teach. But not in high school anymore. That's why I'm studying for my Ph.D."

No one at the table knew what that meant, except Ruth.

Harold Trumpet, amused at their blank expressions, explained, "I expect to be a professor some day and teach in college. When I have my Ph.D., I'll be Dr. Trumpet."

Grandma Birdie was stunned.

"A doctor?" Annie repeated. "Isn't that funny? Ruth is a doctor, too."

Harold Trumpet turned to look at Ruth. "You have a Ph.D.?"

"No," Abel broke in before his sister could reply. "Ruth is a real doctor." His face turned red. "I mean she's a *doctor* doctor."

"A doctor," he said, surprised. "It boggles the mind."

"Do you have some kind of objection to that?" Annie demanded.

He held up his hand. "Hey, wait. Hold your horses. Of course I have no objection. Why should I? It's just that I've never met a woman doctor before. You've got to admit it's a little bit unusual."

"I'm sitting in the same room with a doctor and an almost doctor." Grandma Birdie was impressed. "Wait till everybody hears about this. They'll never believe me."

She sounded as if she couldn't believe it herself.

Harold Trumpet took Ruth's hand in his own again. "Can't you just see people's faces when we go somewhere? 'Folks, look who's here! Dr. Trumpet with his

wife, Ruth, the doctor.' "

Ruth removed her hand gently.

"Can I ask you something?" She went on without waiting for permission. "You're a very personable man. You have a fine career now and ahead of you. Why are you using a matchmaker to find you a wife?"

"I could ask the same thing of you — but I won't," he added with haste as Ruth's eyes narrowed. "I'll tell you. I've been out on lots of dates, but I'm not comfortable. I keep thinking of my brothers and their wives . . ."

Grandma Birdie beamed. "That's nice. You have a big family?"

"Too big. Six brothers and three sisters."

"Your brothers and their wives," Ruth reminded him.

"Oh yes. My three older brothers dated a lot. The girls were wonderful, they said. Then they were married and the girls became wives."

Harold Trumpet almost spat out the word.

Annie was up in arms at once.

"I'm going to be a wife. What's wrong with that?" she demanded.

"Nothing personal," he told her. "It's just that girls ask, wives order."

Ruth's voice when she spoke was icy. "Aren't you taking a terrible chance, then? Why marry at all?"

Grandma Birdie threw her a reproachful glance. "Of course he wants to marry," she said. "Why else would he be here?"

Abel thought he had the answer. "Maybe Mr. Trumpet thinks a matchmaker really knows the people he tries to match. That way there's no guesswork."

Abel felt quite proud of himself. He accepted Hilda's whispered "That's telling them" as his due.

Before anyone else could chime in, the doorbell rang.

Annie leaped to her feet. "That's Bruce. About time, too."

Bruce was not alone.

"Surprise," he called from the doorway. "I've brought a guest."

"*Now* he brings a guest?" Grandma Birdie muttered, but she was by nature too hospitable to turn anyone away.

"Come in, come in," she called, as she began to remove some dishes from the table.

Everyone stared at the newcomer, a man of average size, with curly red hair, twinkling brown eyes, and a smiling pixie face.

"Hi!" Bruce sang out. "I want you to meet my new friend, Dr. John Ralph George."

"Why does he have three first names?" Hilda whispered to Abel. "And why did he have to come now, when things are going so well between Ruth and Mr. Trumpet?"

Grandma Birdie's eyes had glazed over as she studied the newcomer.

"I'm dying," she breathed, as she pressed both hands to her chest. "A doctor and a teacher in my house. *At the same time.*"

Bruce grinned as he urged his friend to sit at the table. To Annie, he whispered, "Grandma Birdie thinks she's died and gone to heaven."

Dr. George refused Grandma Birdie's offer to serve him supper, but he did accept cake and coffee.

"Fantastic," he said, his mouth full. "This cake is so delicious, it's sinful."

Grandma Birdie beamed at him.

"Is he a ham?" Abel asked eagerly. When Bruce nodded, Abel sighed with joy. A real ham, right there in the same room with him.

"I saw Bruce's aerial as I was passing by," Dr. George informed them, between bites. "So naturally I had to meet him."

"I'm sorry about supper, Grandma," Bruce said, though he looked at Annie as he spoke. "We just got to talking, and we forgot the time."

"You're one of those guys who tinkers with amateur radio?" Harold Trumpet asked.

Abel sprang to Dr. George's defense, like a tiger

protecting its young. "You don't know very much about it, do you? Well, for your information, even before you can become a ham, you have to pass a government test. Did you know that?" Without waiting for an answer, Abel rushed on. "Did you know that ham radio is the only hobby controlled by the United States government?"

Harold Trumpet held up his hands. "I surrender," he told Abel. "You're right. If you don't know what you're talking about, and I obviously didn't, you should keep your big mouth shut." He treated Abel to a broad smile. "Are we still friends?"

Abel nodded, and was about to reply when Bruce dropped his bombshell.

"I brought Dr. George on purpose, just to meet Ruth. I told him all about her, and he insisted on coming over. Isn't that something?"

"Just a minute." Harold Trumpet sounded angry. "I thought this was supposed to be my evening."

Grandma Birdie was speechless. *Two* eligible suitors, fighting over her Ruth?

Ruth was obviously stunned.

Hilda kicked Abel under the table to get his attention.

"Are we lucky, or what?" she crowed. "Summer camp, here I come!"

8

It's Not the Last Inning

"Listen," Dr. George said. "If I'm intruding, I'm sorry."

He started to rise from his chair, but Bruce pushed him down again.

"Everybody's welcome here. Right, Grandma?" When she nodded, he went on, "You and Ruth can get together after she and Mr. Trumpet settle matters between them."

Harold Trumpet was still annoyed. "I didn't expect this to be a general meeting. I thought," he said, as he turned to Ruth, "that this was strictly between us. After all, it really doesn't concern anybody else."

"What do you mean, it doesn't concern anybody else?" Abel wanted to know. "Ruth's my sister. And nobody here is a stranger. Except him," he nodded at Dr. George. "But he's a ham, so he's a friend. It's like a brotherhood, sort of," he told Harold Trumpet earnestly. "And we stick together, don't we, Bruce?"

Ignoring the fact that Abel was not a ham, Bruce explained, "Abel is right. That's why John Ralph felt free to drop in on me the way he did, even though we'd never met before."

Dr. George mumbled his agreement through his second large helping of cake.

"And when I heard about Ruth, I couldn't wait to meet her," he said.

"They're fighting over her, Abel." Hilda was ecstatic. No one else heard her, for Ruth had begun to ask Harold Trumpet a question.

"Since you're from a large family, I imagine you want a large family when you marry?"

Abel was quick to note that she had said "when you marry," and not "when we marry."

"Me? You're joking," Harold Trumpet replied. "You can't imagine what it's like to have so many brothers and sisters. There's never a minute's peace. Can you believe that I never had my own room?"

Abel's ears perked up. He gave Harold Trumpet a sympathetic look. Nobody knew what that felt like more than Abel. Now he paid close attention as Harold Trumpet went on.

"I shared a room with two of my brothers. Have you any idea how I longed for some privacy?"

Ruth glanced at Abel. "I can imagine," she said.

Abel was startled. He'd never told Ruth how much

he wanted her room. Annie knew, of course, but Annie wouldn't tell. She respected anything you confided to her as being secret.

"And even though some of my brothers are married, there are still enough of us at home to drive me out of my mind," Harold Trumpet continued. "I see kids all day at school; then there's the hustle and bustle when I come home. What I want, Ruth, and I hope you feel the same way, is a nice, quiet life. And no children," he said with emphasis.

Grandma Birdie was shocked. "No children?" she cried. "What is a marriage without children?"

Harold Trumpet ignored her.

"Think of how it could be," he urged Ruth. "You at your office all day, me at school. And then, at home, peace. We could go away on weekends. In the summer, we could travel during the whole summer vacation period."

Dr. George piped up, "Excuse me, but I don't see how a doctor could take a couple of months off. What would happen to Ruth's practice? She'd lose her patients."

Harold Trumpet glared at him. "Do you mind?" he asked through gritted teeth. "This is a private conversation."

"Bruce and I plan to have a family," Annie put in suddenly. "Children are a blessing."

"Children are a pain in the neck," the teacher shot back. "Take it from me, the expert. I'm with them all day."

Hilda turned to Abel in desperation. "Do something," she commanded. "Or else they'll ruin everything."

"What do you want me to do?" Abel wanted to know. "Send them to the principal's office?"

"Please," Ruth called out, "will you all be quiet and let me have my say?"

Instant silence greeted her remark. Grandma Birdie looked worried; Annie was upset; Bruce and Dr. George seemed amused; Hilda and Abel sat so still they might have been glued to their chairs.

"Harold." Ruth put her hand over his, and didn't try to pull it away when he squeezed it hard. "I think you and I could be friends. You're very personable, and I'm sure you would make an interesting companion."

"I would! I would!" he assured her.

"But . . ."

Harold Trumpet sighed, and released Ruth's hand. "I had a feeling there was a but . . ." His voice trailed off.

"But some day, if and when I marry, I will want to have a family."

Hilda couldn't help interrupting. "But you told Henry Gates you didn't."

Ruth didn't seem to mind Hilda's outburst.

"I told him I wasn't ready for marriage and a *large* family. I didn't say I never wanted a family at all."

She turned back to Harold Trumpet. "The thing is, and I'm sorry if it hurts your feelings," she apologized, "but having you here was not my idea at all."

"Oh no? Then what's he doing here?" he demanded, as he pointed to Dr. George.

Grandma Birdie looked puzzled, but Abel understood. Harold Trumpet thought Dr. George had been invited to act as competition.

"Ruth isn't like that," Abel yelled. "She'd never play a trick like that on you. Ruth doesn't hurt people. Not ever."

"Listen." Dr. George rose. "I seem to have stumbled in on something that's none of my business. I'd better go. I can talk to Ruth another time."

"No," Bruce said

"No," said Harold Trumpet. "I'll go. I wish it had turned out differently. I guess I misunderstood. I thought Mr. Harbinger would have spelled out exactly the kind of person I want to marry."

Abel glared at Hilda, who glanced away. "You and your big, fat ideas," he muttered. "It's all your fault. I

don't know why I let you talk me into things away."

Ruth walked Harold Trumpet to the door, where she shook hands with him. On impulse, she stood on tiptoe and kissed his cheek. "I hope, when you are married, you and your wife will visit. Whoever she is, she'll be lucky to have you."

Abel was proud of his sister. She always tried to soothe someone's hurt.

As soon as the door closed, Dr. George said, "Listen, I only wanted to talk to Ruth briefly. When Bruce told me about her, I thought it would be a good idea to bring her home . . ."

Grandma Birdie was struck dumb. She could only stare at him with shocked eyes.

"No, no," Dr. George hastened to tell her. "It's not what you think. I want her to meet my wife — "

"What?" Annie shrieked. "Your *wife*?"

"Annie," Bruce put in. "Will you just listen? Dr. George and his wife are having a little social gathering tonight at their house. He and a few other doctors meet at each other's homes every Sunday evening."

"And I thought," Dr. George broke in, "that it would be an addition to our group to have the only woman doctor around here."

Ruth's eyes shone. "I'd love to. What a wonderful idea."

After she and Dr. George left, Bruce and Annie

went visiting some friends, and Grandma sat with her ears glued to the radio. Hilda and Abel shared the last piece of pie.

"There goes the ball game," Abel said, downhearted.

"It's not the last inning," Hilda replied. "After all, we still have one more prospect."

9

The Button Man

The next morning, when Abel arrived at Pincher's Grocery, he found Hilda pacing back and forth.

"Tell me what happened," she shouted the moment she spotted him. "When Ruth went to meet the doctor's friends," she added when he seemed puzzled. "Don't just stand there, Abel. Talk."

Abel stared at her with bleary eyes. His head felt heavy; his stomach was grumbling. How did Hilda manage to be so energetic, especially after rising at five A.M. to ride the milkman's horse? Ignoring her, he stumbled into the store, and stumbled out again with one of the fruit stands.

Eyes flashing, Hilda seized Abel's arm.

"Don't you get stubborn with me, Abel Stoner. I have a right to know what's happening. I still want to go to summer camp next year. Or have you forgotten that already?"

Abel fled into the store and staggered out again with the first huge sack of oranges.

"Forget about summer camp," he advised her.

Why does she always have to know everything? he asked himself. He brooded about last night. He and Grandma Birdie stayed up to wait for Ruth to come home. His grandmother was impatient, glaring at the wall clock as if she could force the hands to move a little faster.

"She must be having a nice time," Grandma Birdie said a number of times, "or why would she stay so long? Maybe she met a nice single doctor."

If Ruth was surprised to see them still awake, she didn't mention it. She just smiled, yawned, and said, "I've got to be up early. Good night."

"What's with the good night?" Grandma Birdie was irritated. "You can't tell me at least if you had a good time?"

"Or if I met a nice single doctor?" Ruth's eyes crinkled with amusement. "For the record, Grandma, no." She blew her grandmother a kiss and vanished into her room.

Abel felt cranky. "What's so hard about getting married?" he asked. "People do it all the time."

Grandma Birdie shrugged. "Talking to Ruth is like talking to the wall."

Abel woke from his thoughts of last night when Hilda poked him in the ribs.

"Well," she cried.

"Well nothing. I don't care anymore if Ruth gets married or not. So go away and leave me alone, Hilda. Can't you see that Pincher is watching us through the window?"

Hilda was outraged.

"So let him watch. This is a free country, isn't it? I want to know what you mean, you don't care anymore. You know what's wrong with you, Abel? You give up too easily. So what if your sister turned down two perfectly wonderful prospects. Have you forgotten who's coming on Sunday? He could be the perfect husband."

"You're weird, you know that?" Abel interrupted. "He's sixty years old. He's almost as old as my grandmother. Why would such an old man want to get married?"

"Maybe he needs somebody to take care of him. Or read to him. Or take him to the park on a nice day. Ruth's a doctor. She'd know how to take good care of him."

Abel shook his head, and asked in a patient voice, "Now why would Ruth want to?"

"Because he's rich," Hilda pointed out. "She'd

never have to work again. They could eat in fine restaurants, and go to the country in the summertime. Ruth could buy anything she wanted. She could . . ." Hilda paused. She wasn't sure what rich people did.

Neither was Abel, but he agreed that rich was nice. He even cheered up somewhat.

"Well," he said, finally, "why don't we just wait and see what happens on Sunday?"

On Sunday, they were in for a surprise. The old man was about Grandma Birdie's size, though considerably thinner. He had thick gray hair, smiling blue eyes, and dimples in his cheeks that gave him a permanently cheerful look. He was fast on his feet, darting into the room the moment the door was opened. He handed Grandma Birdie a small bouquet of flowers, and a box of chocolates to Ruth.

"I didn't know about Annie," he apologized, "or I would have brought candy for her, too."

"That's all right, Mr. Fox," Ruth told him. "We'll share this one."

"You'll want to know all about me," George Fox said, as soon as they were seated at the table. "I have a large house, with four bedrooms, two bathrooms, and a big back yard. I live alone, now that my daughters are married and have their own homes."

Four bedrooms. And three of them empty, Abel thought with envy. *Two* bathrooms. He looked at Ruth hopefully, certain she was impressed.

"I am a successful businessman. My wife would want for nothing," he went on.

Every eye was on Ruth now. She didn't seem to notice, just concentrated on her food as if someone might snatch it away before she finished eating.

"Ruth is a doctor," Abel said. "She has her own office and everything."

Everyone waited for Mr. Fox's reaction.

"A doctor, my dear! What a wonderful profession you've chosen. I'm sure you must be a very dedicated person to choose medicine as a career. Especially when it is such a hard uphill battle for a woman. I congratulate you. Your family must be very proud of you."

Grandma Birdie beamed. At last, her expression said, someone who appreciates our Ruth.

Abel glanced at Hilda, who had poked him hard. "See?" She was triumphant. "What did I tell you?"

"And what business are you in?" Annie asked, since it was obvious Ruth wouldn't.

"I'm in buttons. You could say, buttons are my life." He glanced about, giving everyone a glowing smile.

Hilda and Abel stared at one another. Buttons? *Buttons*?

"I can see you're all surprised," George Fox went on. "You're saying to yourselves, what kind of man is this, who gets so excited about buttons? So, let me show you buttons."

He put his hand in his jacket pocket, and then strewed buttons into the center of the table. Some were gold, some silver. Others were colored glass and gleamed like precious gems. There were shell buttons, wooden buttons, ivory buttons, and little pearl buttons. They ranged in size from tiny beads to large coins. Black, white, green, red, blue, pink, yellow — they made a path of colors that glittered from one end of the table to the other.

Everyone reached out to make a choice, hold the buttons in their fingers, turn them round and round, and exclaim over them. Even Abel was caught up in the excitement.

And all the while, George Fox talked.

"Did you know that buttonholes weren't invented until the thirteenth century?" he asked.

"You don't say," Grandma Birdie exclaimed. "Imagine. Not until the thirteenth century."

Abel hid a grin behind his hand. He knew Grandma hadn't the foggiest notion what the words *thirteenth century* meant, but she was impressed anyway.

"And did you know that in the fourteenth century, people wore buttons as ornaments, the way we wear jewelry today? Some people decorated their clothes from the elbow to the wrist. Some people wore them in rows from the neckline to the waist. You could tell who was rich just by looking at the buttons people had. If they wore gold, silver, ivory, or copper buttons, it meant they were not only rich, but important, too."

Abel was amazed, watching Ruth. She seemed to be fascinated by all this information.

"You know so much about buttons, you could write a book about them," Annie exclaimed.

Bruce shrugged. He glanced down at his shirt. He'd never even noticed the buttons before. They seemed quite ordinary to him.

"I thought buttons were just buttons," he said.

Abel agreed, although he remained silent.

George Fox nodded. "For everyday wear, buttons are just buttons. But look at this."

He showed them buttons displayed like fine jewelry in boxes lined with black velvet. "These buttons are made from porcelain. The decorations on them are all hand-painted. They come from France, and Japan."

"So," Ruth said. "Your business is also your hobby. You are a very interesting man, George Fox."

Everyone snapped to attention.

Everyone's eyes shone with sudden hope.

Hilda held her breath.

Abel closed his eyes for a moment, and uttered a silent prayer.

"And you are a wonderful woman, Ruth Stoner. You will make some man very happy one of these days."

Abel's face fell. Hilda frowned. The others at the table carefully avoided looking at one another. These were not the words of a man about to propose marriage.

They were certain when George Fox went on, "You are everything a man could hope for in a wife. But I'm afraid, my dear, that we are not compatible."

Compatible. That was the word George Fox had used in the information he had given Hilda's father. He wanted someone compatible.

"To begin with, I am sixty years old."

Grandma Birdie didn't know what *compatible* meant, but she bristled anyway. "What do you mean, not compatible? My Ruth is as compatible as anybody."

"Of course she is. But I am December, and she is June. I am not looking for a young, beautiful girl. You deserve better than that, Ruth my child. What I need, though, is someone like your grandmother, someone near my own age, someone who can understand me."

Grandma Birdie was so surprised that coffee spilled into her saucer.

"Me? Me?" She laughed uneasily. "You're a man who likes to make a joke of everything, right?"

George Fox shook his head. "No. About this I do

not joke. I told Mr. Harbinger right away. I am a lonely man. I want companionship. At my age, I'm not looking for romance. I leave that to the young people." He smiled at Annie and Bruce, whose hands were entwined on the table. "I want a friend."

He sounded so wistful, Ruth popped up from her chair, kissed the top of his head, and winked at her grandmother. "Listen to him, Grandma," she advised. "It's the best idea I've heard in years. I have to leave now to make some house calls. But I'd like to come back and find you two engaged."

"I'd better leave now, too," the button man said. "I can see Mrs. Stoner is in shock. But I hope, my dear," he leaned across the table to speak earnestly to Grandma Birdie, "I pray you will think over what I've said."

After he left, Annie turned to her grandmother, but before she could speak, Grandma Birdie said, blushing, "A proposal! Can you imagine? He wants to marry *me*."

"Why not?" Annie urged. "I think he's a darling man."

"Don't be ridiculous," Grandma Birdie replied. "People my age don't get married."

"Why?" Abel wanted to know. "Is there a rule about that, too?"

"Marry him, Grandma," Hilda shouted. Her eyes

sparkled. "Do you know what this means?" she asked, when Grandma Birdie and Annie decided to go downstairs to the store.

"What are you talking about?" Abel was annoyed.

Hilda sighed. "Think," she urged. "If Grandma marries George Fox, you could have your own room. You won't have to wait for Ruth anymore. Mr. Fox has a house with *four* bedrooms. One of them could be yours!"

Abel was stunned. Of course. Hilda was right. His dream could come true at last. Not in the way he expected, but still . . . a room of his own.

Then he shook his head. No. Not even for a room of his own. Grandmothers didn't marry. Grandmothers shouldn't marry!

"Listen," he told Hilda firmly, "all I ever asked was, will somebody please marry my sister. Not my *grandmother*! My sister! So do me a big favor. Just forget the whole thing."

10

A Day to Remember

The next morning began a day Abel was certain he would always remember. It started as soon as he arrived at Pincher's Grocery. Hilda was waiting for him. One look at her stubborn expression, the way she stood with hands on her hips, spoiling for an argument, made Abel wonder why he hadn't just stayed in bed.

"You listen to me, Abel Stoner," she said, as soon as he was close enough to hear every word. "It's time for a showdown."

Abel glanced about warily, as if seeking a way to escape. He had seen enough Westerns to know what a showdown was. It was the final confrontation between the good guy in the white hat and the bad guy in the black hat. Of course the good guy always won, but the trouble was that Abel didn't know which one he was.

Before he could utter one word of protest, however,

Mr. Pincher came to the door.

"Are you here again?" he shouted at Hilda. "Talk. Talk. Talk. Do it on your own time, not mine. Abel," he commanded. "Get the fruit stand."

Abel was delighted. He scooted into the store with a triumphant smile. It faded, though, when he saw Hilda still rooted to the sidewalk.

"We talk now, or we talk at lunchtime," Hilda warned.

"Lunchtime, lunchtime," Abel agreed at once. He would agree to anything to make Hilda disappear. So he was grateful when, after giving him a long, considering look, she vanished through the door that led to the apartment over the grocery.

Mr. Pincher kept Abel so busy, he had no time to wonder about the upcoming meeting with Hilda at noon. But when twelve o'clock finally rolled around, he remembered and walked home, dragging his feet.

Hilda gave him a typical greeting. "You want to eat first, or talk first?" she asked, the moment Abel came into the kitchen.

"Let's get this over with," Abel requested. What was the use of preparing one of his favorite jawbreaker sandwiches if Hilda was ready to ruin his appetite?

"I want Grandma to marry Mr. Fox. Now don't interrupt," she warned.

He paid no attention. "This is my house, and if I

want to interrupt I will. You can always go home." He gave her a hopeful look. Maybe she would be angry enough to march to the door. Then he sighed. Not Hilda. When she got an idea in her head, she was worse than a dog worrying a bone.

"You listen to me, and listen hard, Abel. My deal with my father is if I arrange a marriage for one of his clients, I go to summer camp."

"Will you stop telling me things I already know? Don't you ever stop? Ruth just won't get married."

Hilda ignored his remarks. "Who's talking about Ruth?"

Abel's jaw dropped. "You've got a brain like a grasshopper," he said at last. "I thought that's what we were trying to do, get Ruth married."

"My deal," Hilda went on, as if he hadn't spoken, "is that we find a wife for a client. Well, we've found one — Grandma," she finished triumphantly. "Grandma marries Mr. Fox."

"It's like starting a race on one horse and finishing with another," Abel began, but Hilda didn't allow him to continue. She just changed her tactics.

"Abel," she cooed, "just think. You and Grandma and Ruth and Annie could go live in Mr. Fox's house, and you would still have a room all to yourself. And he has two bathrooms! You'd live like a regular rich person. Wouldn't that be great?"

Abel folded his arms and narrowed his eyes. He'd lived with his sisters too long not to recognize the iron will behind the sweet talk.

"No!" To make it more emphatic, Abel said, "Triple times no! I don't want a room in somebody else's house. I want a room in *my* house. Right here. And I don't want my grandmother to get married. I like her just the way she is. So go home, Hilda. I want to have my sandwich *in my own house* and no company." He went to the front door and held it open invitingly. "This way out," he said, giving her a small bow.

Hilda not only refused to leave, she burst into tears. Abel felt stricken. He had known Hilda all her life, and she almost never cried, not stubborn Hilda.

"Don't do that!" he yelled.

Hilda sobbed harder.

Abel came back to the table and stared at her helplessly.

Moments later, Hilda finally took a deep breath, wiped her eyes, and gave Abel a weak smile.

"I knew it wouldn't work," she confessed. "But it was worth a try, anyway."

"Next summer is a long way off," he comforted her. "Maybe your father will send you just the same."

"Well, I can hope, can't I?"

Suddenly, Abel's appetite returned. Now that the squall was over, he could concentrate on building a sandwich. But it was not to be, for footsteps pounding up the stairway announced the arrival not only of his grandmother, but of Annie and Bruce as well.

Hilda and Abel stared at them in astonishment. Usually, Grandma Birdie and Annie snatched a quick snack with Himmel right about now. And Bruce, of course, always had lunch with his father.

"Something's up," Hilda whispered to Abel.

He didn't need her to tell him something was up. It was plain by the set of Annie's lips, by the stubborn look in Bruce's normally gentle eyes, and in the way Grandma Birdie's hands fussed with her apron, then darted to smooth away straying wisps of gray hair, that something was very much up.

Grandma Birdie sank down into one of the kitchen chairs. "So tell me already what couldn't wait till suppertime," she ordered. "Sit down," she added, "it makes me nervous to have you stand over me."

"I don't want to sit down. What I have to say, I'll say standing up," Annie said.

Grandma Birdie gave her an apprehensive look. "It's bad news. I can tell. Somebody died. Somebody died and you want to break the news a little bit at a time."

"Nobody died," Bruce said.

Grandma Birdie could think of only one other possibility. "It's Ruth!" she shrieked. "An accident, right?

Of course! A car accident." She clasped her cheeks with both hands and began to sway back and forth. "They weren't satisfied with horses; they had to go and invent cars. She's in a hospital. That's what you're trying to tell me." Now she clasped her hands and began to beat them against her heart.

The flow of her words was so rapid, no one had been able to interrupt. But now Annie yelled, "GRANDMA!"

Grandma Birdie put a hand across her lips and waited fearfully.

"To begin with," Annie said, "nobody's died, and nobody's been hurt. What Bruce and I want to tell you is this. We're going to get married."

Grandma Birdie sagged in her chair.

"What about the rule?" Abel asked, staring at his grandmother. "The oldest sister has to get married first, remember that rule?"

"What do we do if Ruth never marries? What if she decides to marry when she's thirty, or forty? Where does that leave Bruce and me? We have as much right to live our lives the way we want to as Ruth does."

"We want our own home; we want a family," Bruce said, firmly.

Grandma Birdie shook her head. "You talk like children. What will people say if you get married before Ruth?"

"Who cares what people say?" Abel broke in, grinning. "I think this is one rule that should be broken!"

"So do I," Hilda put in helpfully. Her eyes were glowing. She had never been close up to a bride, had never even been to a wedding. Next to horses, this was probably the most exciting thing that could happen.

Annie took her grandmother's hand in her own. "Grandma," she said in a reasonable voice. "Bruce and I have been going steady for a whole year. Ruth doesn't seem to care about that. So it's up to you. If you say no," she went on, as if she could see the word trembling on her grandmother's lips, "we'll elope."

Grandma Birdie was stunned. "Elope? You wouldn't!"

Annie and Bruce nodded at the same time. "Elope, or get married with everybody at the wedding. It's up to you," Annie repeated.

Grandma Birdie turned to Bruce. "What will your mother and father say?"

"My parents?" Bruce laughed. "Pa has already planned to have the wedding in our back yard. And Ma is going to invite everybody on the block."

"And," Annie rushed in with the rest of the news, "they've rented a nice little one-bedroom apartment for us, only two blocks away."

Grandma Birdie paled. "Already?" she cried.

"When is all this going to happen?"

"In two weeks," Annie and Bruce chorused happily together.

Everyone agreed it was a beautiful and dramatic wedding. For as Annie stood next to Bruce, glowing in her mother's wedding dress, the summer sky began to darken. At first crickets provided the only music. But then a storm filled the air with crackling background sounds. Soon flashes of lightning streaked earthward with jagged brilliance.

When Abel, as best man, handed Bruce the ring, he glanced apprehensively at the sky. Bruce winked at him.

"We'll make it, pal," he whispered. "Not to worry."

He was right. The ceremony was over just as the first warning drops of rain began to fall.

Everyone ran laughing and shrieking for cover to the Jonas apartment.

"Look at that wedding cake!" someone called out.

"Don't cut it," another guest said. "It would be a shame to cut into such a beautiful cake."

Grandma Birdie glowed. She hadn't approved of the wedding. It went against the rule. But she loved Annie and Bruce. Could she allow them to get married, and not provide the traditional wedding cake? Could she bear to have someone else bake that special cake?

"Grandma," Abel asked her later, "I never thought you'd bake the cake. How come you did?"

She patted his hand.

"Abel, there is a time to be stubborn, but also a time to give in. Do I want Annie and Bruce to start their married life with a quarrel? What would be the use of that?" She looked off into space, her mind clearly elsewhere for the moment. Then she patted Abel's hand again.

"I have lost enough people in my life. Do you think I want to lose them, too? No. I'm not that foolish."

She gave him an impish grin. "Like you said, Abel. Sometimes a rule is made to be broken, right?"

Sometime during the evening, Annie and Bruce slipped away, to have a one-day honeymoon at Coney Island.

When the summer rain ceased, the guests began to leave. As they walked home, Grandma Birdie and Ruth chatted, exchanging details about the wedding. Abel was silent.

Back in their own apartment, he glanced around. Strange, Abel thought. Annie would live only minutes away. She would be back in the coffee shop and the bakery Monday morning. But already he missed her.

He wondered whether he would miss Ruth, too, one day.

Leaning back on the couch, he ignored Ruth and

Grandma, who were having one last cup of coffee in the kitchen. He sighed. It had been a beautiful wedding. He was delighted that Bruce and Annie were so happy at last. But wouldn't it have been even more wonderful if it had been the right sister who had married?

11

Ruth Makes a Decision

"Summer is almost over," Hilda wailed. "What's taking Grandma so long to say yes?"

She and Abel were in his kitchen, having lunch. Hilda's sandwich was generous, stuffed with vegetable cream cheese and large, ripe black olives. But it wasn't the masterpiece that Abel had concocted — a huge slice of pumpernickel bread, carefully spread with a combination of ketchup, sour cream, and a hint of fiery horseradish, filled with large chunks of pickled herring, sliced onions, and radishes, with a final sprinkling of sunflower seeds, over which the second slice of pumpernickel struggled to stay in place.

Hilda had to wait for Abel to chew and swallow his first mouthful of food before he could reply. He licked some of the sour cream from his fingers, meanwhile giving her a sidelong glance that made Hilda instantly suspicious.

"Well, is it yes?" she asked.

Abel shook his head. He knew his answer would drive Hilda mad, but he felt good about it.

"It's no."

Hilda still clung to a bit of hope. "Is it a maybe no, or a hundred percent no?"

"It's a big, fat NO. In capital letters." Abel prepared to take another bite of sandwich, but Hilda grabbed his arm.

"Why?" she cried. "She *likes* him. Ruth likes him. Annie likes him. You like him. Hasn't she let Mr. Fox come here every night for supper this past month? Hasn't she been going out with him, like a steady date?"

Abel nodded.

"Then it's not fair!"

"You're not worried about Grandma. You just want to go to your old summer horse camp. That's all you're interested in. Horses!" Abel sniffed.

Hilda studied Abel for a long, thoughtful moment. "You don't know the first thing about horses, Abel. Maybe it's time for you to meet one, face to face."

"What for?" Abel was surprised. "I don't care about horses."

"Maybe it's because you're afraid."

Abel was insulted. "Me? Afraid? That's a laugh."

"Then prove it," she challenged. "Meet me tomorrow morning — "

"Meet you at five o'clock in the morning?" he interrupted. "To look at a horse? You've got to be joking."

"So you are afraid." She sounded triumphant. "You're a coward, Abel Stoner."

Abel's face purpled with anger. He ought to haul off and swat her. He would if she were a boy. But he could imagine Grandma Birdie's horrified reaction if he struck Hilda: "You hit a *girl*? In my house?"

For sure, Grandma Birdie would have a rule about that. So, controlling himself with an effort, he told Hilda in icy tones, "I'll be there."

He was relieved that Hilda had the good sense to leave it at that, was even smart enough to go home, so that Abel could finish his lunch in peace. But somehow the sandwich no longer appealed to him.

Girls, he brooded. Horses. Who needed them? Yet true to his word, Abel was out of the house in the predawn quiet of the new day. He was surprised at the quality of the silence, broken only by the distant clip-clop of the milkman's horse, and, here and there, the faint chirps of birds that made small punctuation marks of sound in the stillness.

Abel took a deep breath. The air felt fresh and clean,

newly washed by the rain that fell during the night. Overhead, a whisper of a half moon clung to the sky, reluctant to make way for the barest hint of light in the eastern sky.

Savoring this moment, Abel ambled toward Pincher's Grocery, listening to the soft *tap-tap* of his shoes against the sidewalk.

Strange, how different everything was at this hour. Was this how Hilda felt when she slipped out of her apartment, alone but not lonely?

As though she sensed his mood, Hilda greeted him quietly. Then she led the way to the next block, where the milkman's horse waited with drooping head.

"Hello, Big Boy," she whispered, reaching out to stroke his side.

"Big Boy?" Abel repeated. "What kind of a name is that for a horse?"

"Horses don't care what they're called, only how you treat them, isn't that right, you beautiful thing?"

Big Boy responded with a whinny, a gentle neighing sound of recognition. He turned his head and looked at Hilda with his large, soft, brown eyes. Hilda held out a lump of sugar, which he took daintily from her palm.

Hilda handed Abel a lump of sugar. "Go ahead, feed it to him," she urged. "Big Boy loves sugar."

Abel took the sugar gingerly, then stared at Big

Boy. He hadn't realized how large an animal a horse was. In Western movies, cowboys leaped off and on horses with ease. Horses seemed smaller on the big screen. Up close, Abel felt as ill at ease as if Big Boy were an elephant.

Following Hilda's instructions, however, he opened his palm and held out the lump of sugar. He didn't dare admit to Hilda that he felt almost paralyzed with fear. Suppose Big Boy bit him? His teeth looked sharp, especially when Big Boy pulled back his lips. Abel closed his eyes tight, and waited. There was a gentle lick, a wet palm where the horse's tongue had touched it, and the sugar was gone. When Hilda offered Abel another lump of sugar, he refused.

Horses, Abel told himself, were great in the movies, but that was as close as he ever wanted to come to them ever again.

"Now we'll ride him," Hilda announced.

Big Boy seemed to grow in size when Abel sat astride him. If only Big Boy were a pony!

Hilda didn't seem to notice Abel's discomfort, nor his obvious relief when they began to walk home again.

The outing had given Abel a lot to think about. Back home, stretched out on the couch once more, Abel recalled the gentleness with which Hilda had spoken to Big Boy, how lovingly she had stroked him, with what delight she had ridden him. For the first time, Abel began to understand why Hilda was so desperate to attend a summer horse camp.

Unaccustomed to rising so early in the morning, Abel fell asleep, to wake to the sound of angry voices.

"Grandma," his sister Ruth was saying as Abel's eyes popped open. "You don't understand. I'm not asking you. I'm telling you."

They must have been having an argument while Abel was asleep. Confused, Abel asked, "You're not asking Grandma what, Ruth?"

His sister turned on him irritably. "Another country heard from," she snapped.

"Hey," he objected. "What are you mad at me for?"

Ruth was apologetic. "I'm sorry, Abel. I'm just trying to get Grandma to recognize that I'm a grown woman, and that I can be trusted to make my own decisions."

"You know what she wants?" Grandma Birdie demanded. "She wants to take a job in a hospital—Fordham Hospital. *In the Bronx*," Grandma Birdie almost shouted. She made it sound like the end of the world instead of just an hour's ride on the subway.

Abel was dazed. "You want to move out, Ruth? Give up your office and everything?"

Ruth's face took on a glow Abel had never seen before. "I've been offered a wonderful opportunity,

Abel. Through the doctors I met. One of them heard Fordham wanted a doctor to work in the emergency room. The job includes room and board. Oh, Abel, the experience it will give me! I couldn't learn as much in a lifetime in my own office."

Grandma Birdie looked so stricken, Abel was sorry for her. *I guess when you're old,* he thought, *it's hard to accept new ideas.* And Ruth in an emergency room in a hospital was very hard to accept.

"Bruce should never have brought that doctor friend here. That's what started this whole thing," Grandma Birdie muttered.

"He did me a tremendous favor, Grandma. Since I've been part of that group of doctors, I've had the kind of social life I enjoy, with people who talk the same language. And if it hadn't been for Bruce, and then this group, I'd be standing still instead of learning more." Ruth laughed. "The funny thing is, not even my doctor friends thought I would actually take the job. But they were glad for me when I did."

Grandma Birdie seemed not to have heard. "What will people say?" she whispered.

Before Ruth could reply, Abel said, "Grandma. You can't keep telling everybody what to do. You were against Annie and Bruce getting married. And you know what? They did, and the world didn't come to an end. Now you're trying to tell Ruth what to do. But nobody can tell you what to do, can they?"

Grandma Birdie was taken by surprise. "*Me*?"

"Sure. We're all telling you to marry Mr. Fox, but you won't," Abel went on swiftly, before she could break in. "Because you say you like your life the way it is."

Grandma Birdie nodded.

"But at first you didn't let Annie and Bruce live the way they wanted to. Until they forced you to let them. And now you see how happy they are. Tell the truth, Grandma. Have you ever seen two happier people?"

Grandma Birdie studied him, sent an appealing glance at Ruth, and then, because she was honest, admitted, "I was wrong. I shouldn't have stood in their way so long."

"And if it had been up to you, Ruth would never have become a doctor, right?"

"You tell her, kid," Ruth cheered him on.

"But she is, and she did it the hard way, with everybody against the idea. And now Fordham Hospital in the Bronx thinks enough of Ruth to offer her a wonderful opportunity. And you want to stand in her way, like you did with Annie and Bruce. You were wrong once, Grandma. Maybe you're wrong now, too. End of speech," he said abruptly.

Grandma Birdie sat down, as if she had suddenly become weary, although it was early in the morning.

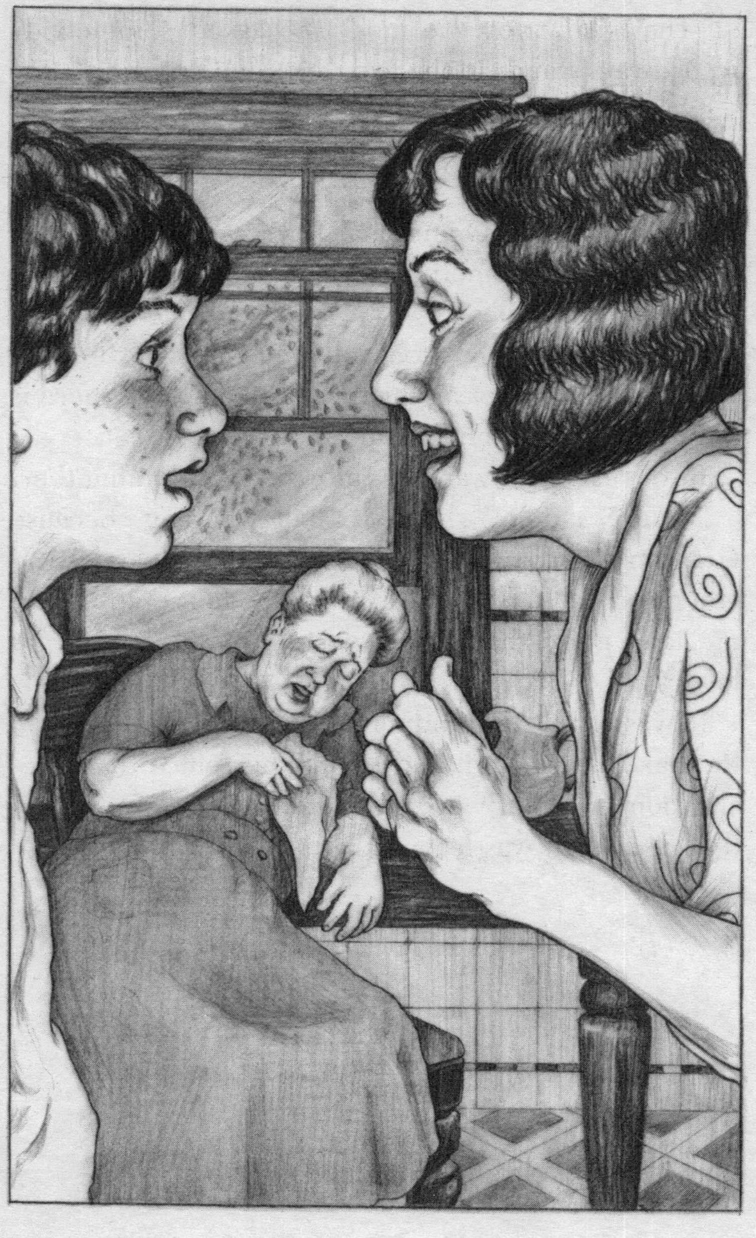

"That's how you see me?" she asked. "Somebody who always stands in the way? No, don't answer." She held up her hand. "You once told me, Abel, that this is Brooklyn, New York, in the United States of America."

"He was right, Grandma," Ruth said gently. "You have rules, but sometimes, when the world changes, there are new rules."

"So maybe I'm not too old to change a little bit," Grandma said, after a long pause. "I suppose there is a time to control, and a time to let go."

Ruth rushed forward to embrace her grandmother.

"You're a doll," she said, half weeping, because Grandma Birdie's eyes were filled with tears. "And you don't have to worry, Grandma. You're not losing me, any more than you've lost Annie. We'll always love you."

It wasn't until Grandma Birdie had gone down to the bakery and Ruth had left for her office that a realization hit Abel with the sudden force of a roll of thunder. Ruth was leaving!

12

A Door Closes

"Listen, Abel," Ruth said. They were in her room. She talked as she packed in her quick, efficient way. Although she seemed calm, Abel knew Ruth was excited and happy.

"You can keep my furniture, or sell it to the second-hand man and buy whatever you prefer."

Abel's reply was prompt. "I want your desk. And the bookcase."

She smiled. "Good choice."

Abel closed his eyes and dreamed. He'd have a desk! No more school books and papers spread out on the kitchen table while he did his homework. No more clearing everything away so a meal could be served. No, sir! He could leave his things scattered about. His bag of marbles, his top, and some of his games would fit into one of the desk drawers. His comic books and all his Horatio Alger books would be within easy reach on the bookshelves. The collection of shells Bruce had given him as a birthday gift one year would look great spread out on top of the bookcase.

Best of all, he'd have space for a shelf on the wall opposite the door for his ham radio. Bruce had promised to help Abel buy the necessary parts and show him how to build his radio set. Grandpa Stoner's map of the world would hang in the center of the wall, surrounded by all the cards that would flood in from other hams, after he took his government exam, of course.

He'd buy a second-hand chair, a small one, so that he could sit and read in quiet and peace when Grandma Birdie listened to her favorite radio programs at night.

Everything he now stored in a cardboard box in the hall closet would finally be handy.

And hams could visit, *would* visit. They'd sit around and swap stories . . .

"Abel." Ruth tapped his shoulder. "Wake up. You'll have lots of time to dream after I leave." Before he could speak, she added, "I'm sorry you had to wait so long for this room."

"You knew! But I never said anything to you."

At that moment, Hilda arrived, her mouth set in a grim line. She was angry with Ruth, and told her so.

"It just isn't fair, Ruth. Grandma isn't going to marry Mr. Fox. And you didn't get married. Now I won't be able to go to summer camp next year."

"Yes you will," Abel assured her. "Your father always gives in."

Hilda shook her head. "Not when we have a deal. He says I have to learn that if I make a deal, I have to stick to it, win or lose."

"I'm sorry, Hilda," Ruth said. "But people aren't puppets. They have their own dreams. I don't think you really expected me to marry to make a wish come true for you."

Hilda admitted, "I guess deep down I always knew it wouldn't happen. Not with you. But why can't Grandma get married? She *likes* Mr. Fox."

"Don't give up hope," Ruth told her. "Grandmothers have been known to change their minds."

"I don't know what your problem is. You've still got the milkman's horse," Abel pointed out.

"Don't be so dumb, Abel. That's not riding."

Ruth studied Hilda's downcast face and sighed.

"Listen, Hilda," she said. "Since your grand plan to get me married didn't work, I'll make it up to you a little, all right?"

Hilda and Abel looked at her expectantly.

"How would you like to take riding lessons once a week at the riding academy near Prospect Park? For one month. I'll pay for the lessons."

Hilda gasped.

"*Riding* lessons?" she repeated, sounding dazed. "For a whole month?"

"It's a start. After that, it's up to you."

Hilda began to think out loud. "Maybe Grandma will let me help in the bakery after school. I can help kids with their homework, and charge them. Oh, Ruth!"

She flung herself across the room to give Ruth a bear hug.

"I'm going home to tell my father. Riding lessons," she caroled and spun out the door.

"That was nice, Ruth," Abel told her. "Hilda is really wild about horses."

"I can understand. She feels about horses the way I feel about being a doctor. And now," she reminded him, "your wish is coming true. And," she added, with a mischievous smile, "you didn't have to have somebody please marry your sister to get it, did you?"

"You think you'll ever get married?" Abel wondered.

"I don't know. Maybe. Maybe not. Let's not try to predict the future, Abel." Ruth glanced at her watch. "Look at the time! I have to leave right now."

She hugged Abel.

"What about Grandma — "

"Don't worry, Abel. I'll stop in the bakery to say goodbye to her and Annie."

SODA FOUNT
MORRIS THE TAILO

After she left, Abel moved about in Ruth's room as if he were making a voyage of discovery. He touched the walls, gazed out the window, pulled the shade up and down, and flicked the overhead light on and off.

As if in a dream, he walked to the door and closed it carefully.

I'm not crying, he told himself, as he brushed away tears that had welled up in his eyes. *I'm not*!

Softly, as if someone could overhear him, he said aloud, "So this is what it feels like to close a door on a room of my own."